PRAISE FOR THE L
MYSTERY SE

"A smart, snarky series… Cozy mystery readers will adore Larkin Day."

BOOKLIFE, EDITOR'S PICK

"…an entertaining whodunit with a captivating amateur sleuth."

KIRKUS REVIEWS

"Ode to Murder is refreshing, and definitely recommended for fans of a good mystery. But it's also a great read for anyone who, like Larkin, is searching for a new story that can reach them in surprising, unexpected ways."

INDIEREADER

LIKE, SUBSCRIBE, AND MURDER

LIKE, SUBSCRIBE, AND MURDER

A LARKIN DAY MYSTERY
BOOK 2

NICOLE DIEKER

Like, Subscribe, and Murder is a work of fiction. The characters, incidents, and dialogue are creations of the author's imagination or are used fictitiously. Any resemblance to actual events or persons, living or dead, is entirely coincidental.

Copyright © 2023 by Nicole Dieker

All rights reserved. No part of this book may be reproduced in any form or by any electronic or mechanical means, including information storage and retrieval systems, without written permission from the author, except for the use of brief quotations in a book review.

Cover design and interior design by Alan Lastufka.

First Edition published January 2023.

10 9 8 7 6 5 4 3 2 1

ISBN 978-1-7336919-7-0

For Alan, who took a chance on Larkin.

CHAPTER 1

"Are you ready to do it ALL AGAIN?"

Larkin was not ready. She had told herself she was ready, the first time Anni had suggested she sign up for guided fitness classes. Those three words, in that particular order, had made the whole thing sound achievable. Larkin would exchange her hard-earned barista money—"don't worry," Anni had said, "it's sliding-scale"—for a class in which a guide would nudge her gently towards fitness. A hand on her lower back, whispering affirmations as Larkin dangled her fingers six inches above her toes.

The Pratincola fitness complex might have offered that class, somewhere.

It was not the class they were currently taking.

"I said, ARE YOU READY?"

Larkin was supposed to respond. She was supposed to have enough space, between each rapid and ragged breath, to shout "I'm ready!" while simultaneously bouncing from one foot to the other in what their guide called a *rest motion*. They rested, if anyone besides their guide could call it that, in between each set—which, in this particular section, had included squats, lunges, push-ups, reverse push-ups, jumping jacks, burpee sprints, and some kind of running-in-place exercise called *high knees*.

"Face your buddy," their guide had said, "and see who can get their knees the highest!"

If it had been any of their previous guided fitness sessions, Larkin would have been facing Anni—and since Larkin was built like a triple-scoop ice cream cone and Anni was built like a carrot stick, Larkin could have won the contest without having to make an effort. Larkin's knees were always higher than Anni's, even when they were sitting next to each other on Anni's sofa and discussing Larkin's future career as Pratincola's newest— "and only!" Anni had said—private detective. But this time, Anni was at the front of the room, bouncing cheerfully next to a sweating, resolute woman whose recalcitrant son sat in the corner and played on his phone.

This time, Larkin's buddy was Ed Jackson, Assistant Professor of Music at Howell College, director of the Pratincola Concert Choir, and kinda-sorta-maybe her boyfriend.

Larkin had not been ready for this either—and she didn't know whether to blame this one on Anni, who had invited Ed to join them at guided fitness; her mother, who had initially urged Larkin to join Ed's choir; or Ed himself, who had continued to show an interest in Larkin even after the two of them had found a dead body together. Even after Thanksgiving dinner with Larkin's mother (who just happened to be the dean of Howell and kinda-sorta Ed's boss) and Larkin's mother's girlfriend Claire (who just happened to be a police officer). Even after a second Thanksgiving dinner with Ed's family, with better food and a bigger table and only a single joke about Larkin being the only white person in the room.

She didn't know if Ed had only asked her to his family's Thanksgiving because she had asked him to hers—and that had been a mistake, they had just kissed for the first time, she had thought they were ready to celebrate holidays together and they hadn't been.

Because Ed hadn't invited her to his family's Christmas.

But he had kissed her again, at midnight, on New Year's Eve.

The two of them had celebrated at Ben and Mitchell's mansion—Ed and Larkin had spent a lot of time with Ben and Mitchell that fall, since Ben was writing an opera and needed both Ed's musical expertise and Larkin's theater experience—and on New Year's Eve the two gentlemen hosted a formal dinner, starting with cocktail hour and ending with imported Champagne. Ben played hostess, ensuring that everyone had something to drink and someone to talk to. Larkin had wanted to talk to Ed, but Ben had seated them at opposite ends of the shimmering dining room table, citing some rule of etiquette that suggested Larkin would be better paired with one of Mitchell's business partners. Larkin had spent the entire dinner recapping her former theater career, her work as an assistant director in New York, her stalled dissertation, her interest in Chekhov and Sondheim and Shakespeare. Mitchell's business partner asked her several questions about *Romeo and Juliet*, beginning with "Does the play work when it is set in modern day?" and ending with "Do you think that *Romeo and Juliet* were truly in love, or were they merely two young people who had been failed by a decaying society? If they had been given the opportunity to become adults, would they have made the same decisions?"

"Don't worry," Ben whispered, passing behind Larkin to access one of the mansion's many bathrooms. "I'll make sure you get your kiss at midnight."

He'd done it, too—leading Ed and Larkin to an enclosed patio he called *the grotto* and handing each of them a champagne flute.

"You'll be able to hear all of us calling out the numbers," Ben said. "The pool's heated, so feel free to get comfortable. I'll make sure nobody comes in—or out, as the case may be."

Then he laughed. He was a little drunk. "It's my turn to be on the case! Larkin, do you think I'll be as good a detective as you?"

He kissed them both—on the cheeks, naturally—and left them to figure out how to stay warm until the year ended.

That evening, magical as it was, already felt like *then*. Now it was Monday, January 30, the last week of the first month of the new year. Larkin and Ed were kissing on a regular basis, and she'd spent Saturday night and Sunday morning at his apartment, wearing a sweatshirt she had borrowed from her mother and then taking it off. But Larkin wasn't sure she could call Ed her boyfriend. She had no idea what he wanted, or whether it was appropriate to ask him what he wanted. The two of them had stopped talking about those kinds of things after Thanksgiving, and they hadn't started talking about them again— even though Ben and Mitchell's New Year's Eve party should have given them more than enough resolve—and Larkin wasn't sure why.

Which was why she was trying so hard to get her knees higher than Ed's, even though Ed was the kind of person who went to the fitness center every day and Larkin was the kind of person who didn't even know which classes were available.

"I'm ready!" Ed shouted, his clear tenor carrying to the front of the room.

I'm ready, Larkin mouthed, even though she wasn't.

———

After class they all lunged for their phones, even though the class was only 45 minutes long and they had already completed nearly a hundred lunges. IF it had been any other day, Larkin would have made the joke aloud, to Anni, and her petite, precise friend would have said "There were exactly 96. Four sets of 24." But Anni had her head bent over a device of her own—something small and boxy and open-source—and was tapping rapidly with the second and third fingers of her right hand.

"Great job today, Larkin!" It was the guide, a young woman named Bonnie Cooper. "You were working extra hard, I could tell."

"Thanks," Larkin said, pulling her long, dark ponytail away from the back of her neck and wondering if Anni had brought an extra towel. Bonnie was the only person in the room who wasn't sweating, even though she had done the same 96 lunges as everyone else while simultaneously giving instructions and encouragements from the tiny pink headset that was still strapped to her face.

The current conversation, Larkin understood, was another *encouragement*. "Do you mind if we get a picture?" Bonnie said, holding up a phone that matched her headset. "My subs need to see real people, you know? I want them to understand that *anyone* can do this."

At first, Larkin assumed that Bonnie was referring to

some kind of substitute fitness instructor crowd. Then, as Bonnie pulled her in for a quick embrace, instructed her to smile, held the phone in front of them, and began snapping selfies, Larkin realized that Bonnie was probably referring to her *subscribers*—which meant that the photos, in which Bonnie looked *aspirational* and Larkin looked *real*, were likely to end up on one of Bonnie's social media profiles. Or, more likely, all of them. "I'm *Blithe and Bonnie* on social," she would say at the beginning and end of every class, their own little version of *namaste*.

"Hello, new student!" Bonnie continued, calling out to Ed. "I'm Bonnie Cooper."

"Ed Jackson," Ed said, as Bonnie put her arm around him and began taking more pictures. "I've seen you in the weight room," she said, clicking and filtering and resizing. "What brought you into my class?"

"She did," Ed said, gesturing to Larkin. This meant that Larkin got to watch Bonnie look up from her phone, take in Ed's muscular figure and shining brown skin, glance at Larkin's not-very-muscular figure and red, sweaty face, and reassess the situation. "Nice work, Larkin!"

"Actually, it was Anni who invited him."

"Who?"

"Anni Morgan." Larkin had been a teacher, once. She had taught undergraduates during the brief period of time when she was a theater graduate student, before transitioning away from theater and academia to whatever-she-was-now. A barista, on her tax returns. A detective, in the conversations she and Anni would have—"business planning sessions," Anni would say—while drinking coffee and herbal tea in Anni's apartment. An Iowan, maybe, still living in the house her mother had bought after moving to Pratincola and becoming Dean Day, in a room that she and her mother still referred to as *the guest bedroom*.

But when she had been a teacher—even though it felt like it had happened a long time ago—it had been exactly the same way. She could never remember the names of the students like Anni, the ones who showed up and did the work and never caused trouble. She could only remember the names of the students who were struggling; the ones who got red-faced when it was their turn to take the stage and had sweat stains under their armpits by the end of their soliloquies.

"Which one is Anni?"

Larkin scanned the room. In most cases, she would have said *the one with the pixie cut* or *the one with the glasses*, but this time the distinguishing factor was even more obvious. "She's the only one still on her phone."

"Anni!" Ed called out, and Anni looked up. Then she looked back at her phone again, did a quick flutter with her index and middle fingers, and put the device in her bag. "Sorry," she said, putting the bag over her shoulder and joining the group. "I mean—"

Anni, who made her living as a freelance writer, rarely had trouble finding an appropriate word—but Larkin watched her evaluate several options and dismiss them all. "Sorry," she said again. Her cheeks reddened slightly, but not from exertion; the corners of her mouth twitched like she was trying to suppress a smile.

"Hello, Anni!" Bonnie said, in a way that suggested she was doing some kind of teacher mnemonic trick in her head, *Anni with the Peter Pan haircut* or something like that. "Good to see you again." She did not ask Anni if she could take her picture. Instead, she turned back to Ed and Larkin —most of her gaze resting on Ed, naturally—and said "You're okay if I share these on social, right?"

"Sure," Ed said.

Larkin was less sure, but it didn't matter—Bonnie had

launched the images into the internet, never to be unseen again.

As Larkin, her maybe-sorta boyfriend, and her definitely best friend picked up their bags and towels and water bottles and left the fitness classroom, Bonnie—who was pulling off her pink headset with one hand and pulling at her phone screen with the other, said "Ed! We've already gotten 34 likes! One new sub! They *love* Ed content at *Blithe and Bonnie!*"

Then Larkin remembered that there was another category of students whose names were impossible to forget—and Ed was the only person in the room who fit that category. She watched him look at Bonnie, and then she watched him look at her, and she understood that he was having a similar realization. Maybe he had it all the time. Maybe, for Ed, it was less of a realization than a reality.

"I wasn't ready to become *content*," Ed said, reaching for Larkin's hand as they left the building—but it was January, in Eastern Iowa, and Larkin was wearing a pair of gloves so thick there was no space for them to interlace their fingers.

"I wasn't ready for any of this," Larkin said. "We'll say it's all Anni's fault, okay?"

"Sure," Ed said, and they both turned towards Anni—who had, somewhere between the steps of the fitness complex and the snow-shoveled parking lot, disappeared.

CHAPTER 2

Larkin did not, for one minute, assume that Anni was lost. Anni was not the kind of person who got lost. Anni was the kind of person who always knew where she was, and where she was going next, and how to color-code her upcoming appointments on her perpetually updating calendar.

Plus they had just seen her, like, *twenty seconds ago.*

But if Larkin really was going to become a private detective and not another failed theater artist whose greatest contribution to the artistic world was the ability to draw a leaf on a latte, she had to treat every potential situation as a potential mystery.

"Do you think she slipped on the ice?" There wasn't much ice, and most of it was covered in the kind of blue salt that stuck to Larkin's boots and deposited itself on the floor of Larkin's mother's kitchen, but the best theater artists followed their instincts and the best private detectives followed their hunches—which meant Larkin would follow the first idea that came to mind, even if she was pretty sure it wasn't the right one.

"She's probably still inside, talking to someone," Ed said. This, Larkin knew, was *definitely* not the right idea. Anni didn't talk, not in the way that other people did. She conveyed information, and then she was silent. There was absolutely no chance that Anni was still inside the Pratincola fitness complex, chitter-chattering to somebody about the weather or the football or whatever it was Eastern Iowans discussed in January. Probably not corn. Larkin had only lived in Iowa for six months, but even she knew it was too early to talk about corn.

So she scanned her immediate surroundings, looking for clues. There were no Anni-sized footprints, anywhere around them—but that was probably because the sidewalks had been shoveled a few days ago, and it hadn't snowed since. There were no Anni-sized indentations in any of the piles of muddy snow that had been plowed into the corners of the parking lot. There were plenty of cars in the lot—it was New Year's Resolution season, after all— and Larkin made a mental note of how easy it was to distinguish between the cars that came from garages and the cars that came from driveways. This could prove useful, in a future investigation. *The suspect must have parked the car in a garage, overnight! Start searching all of the houses that have garages!*

Unfortunately, it was not proving useful in this one.

"Hey, I should go," Ed said. "Do you want to get together for lunch tomorrow?"

"Sure," Larkin said, still looking at the parking lot. She had watched the sunset, through the fitness complex windows, between their third and fourth sets of burpee sprints. There were lights, of course—the entire building was lit up like the Christmas tree that Larkin and her mother had yet to take down—but there were just enough shadows to turn details into secrets. There was a car, for example, with Illinois plates and enough bumper stickers to suggest the driver wanted to communicate not only *where they were going* but also *where they had been*—and as Larkin took two steps forward to see if she could get a lock on the driver's philosophies, she heard the double beep indicating that Ed had unlocked his car.

"I'll see you at the coffee shop at noon," Ed said, and Larkin turned and waved, and then realized that what she really ought to do was run the few steps to Ed's car and embrace him, give him the chance to kiss her cheek if he wanted to, all of the sweat on her face had dried up in the cold Midwestern air so it wouldn't be gross or anything like that, plus if he really was her boyfriend he shouldn't mind kissing her even if she were sweaty, and maybe that would be one more clue to help her decide what they were to each other, and—

But Ed's door was closed, and his car was backing slowly out of its parking space, and when he waved one more time through the driver-side window, it was not meant for Larkin.

It was meant for Anni, who had reappeared next to Larkin *as if by magic*—and who, as they continued their walk from the Pratincola fitness complex to Anni's apartment building, made absolutely no mention of where she had gone.

Instead, she launched right into the business at hand—their weekly business planning session.

"I know we were hoping to launch before the holidays, but it's really better this way," she explained, as the two of them navigated the seasonably early darkness and the sections of sidewalk that were still clumped over with snow. Larkin was wearing the coat her mother had bought when she moved from the Pacific Northwest to the unfamiliar Midwest; it was ten years old and roughly the size of an inflatable mattress. This was one of the reasons why she had been hoping to launch her new business before the holidays—to start earning more money and stop wearing her mother's clothing.

But Anni had argued—probably correctly—that they weren't ready. "Your tax returns are going to be so much easier," she said. "Not that you won't have all kinds of extra forms to fill out this year, since you'll be filing partial year taxes for both California and Iowa, but the last thing you need is an extra Schedule C, especially since you'll show a loss instead of a profit and you'll have to write a letter to the IRS explaining why your private detective agency should be considered a business instead of a hobby."

They had discussed, before the holidays, whether Larkin's business-not-hobby could effectively be called an *agency*, since the only person who would be effectively employed by the business was Larkin. "I'll be your pro-bono consultant," Anni said. "Probably your pro-bono accountant as well, except I'm not a CPA so I can only really call myself a *financial advisor*. I can also help you promote, if you want."

"Yes," Larkin had said, the two of them side-by-side on Anni's sofa, cream-and-sugar coffee next to lemon-ginger tea. "We need to tell everyone that I am available to solve murders."

"It can't just be murders," Anni said. "You're never going to make a profit if you have to wait for people in Pratincola to murder each other. Plus that's kind of like wishing people would die, and wishing other people would kill them, and I don't think either of us really want to do that." She transferred her mug of tea to a coaster and began tapping on her laptop. "You need to learn how to solve everything."

the kitchen to the dimly lit living room sofa; to kneel, without hesitation, on the center cushion; to reach out with two fingers and—this is where Larkin saw her mother pause, her imagination filling in the gap she was about to create—peek between the window blinds.

"She's still there," Larkin's mother said, restoring the blinds and returning to the kitchen. "I just saw her walk by."

"I saw her when I pulled in," Larkin said. Officer Claire Novak, out of uniform; the pashmina Josephine had given her for Christmas just barely visible under her puffy coat. Walking her aging golden retriever, Pal, as if it were a perfectly normal thing to do on a Monday evening. Around and around and around the block, as Josephine was now walking around and around and around the table.

"What does it mean?" Larkin's mother asked again. This was even more out of character than the anxiety; Larkin had grown up listening to her mother explain—first to her students, and then to Larkin herself, when her mother had determined she was old enough—that every well-constructed sentence had both a connotation and a denotation. A text and a subtext, stated and understated.

Then Larkin understood. "It means *you*."

Josephine and Claire had been together since October. In November, Claire set up a spare toothbrush in the bathroom. In December, Josephine asked her daughter to add *kibble* and *lint rollers* to their online shopping list. On New Year's Eve, the three of them had taken turns with the hair dryer and the mirrors, donning sequins and jackets for their respective parties. Josephine and Claire were making stops at both academic and law enforcement gatherings, and there were jokes about towns and gowns—even though Larkin, dressing for Ben and Mitchell's mansion, was the only one of them wearing a dress.

"Wow," Ed had said, when he arrived to pick up Larkin. "You look amazing—and so do you, Officer Novak."

Josephine had let her daughter and her girlfriend use the bathroom first; she arrived in the living room just in time to hear Claire say—with a smile—"Thanks, Dr. Jackson."

"She doesn't like it when people call her *Officer*," Josephine had said, and Larkin watched her mother put her arm around this woman who had, already, become an integral part of their lives.

"Not when I'm off duty, anyway," Claire had said.

"I'm never off duty," Josephine had said. She had asked Claire, a few weeks ago, whether it was all right to begin presenting themselves as a couple. "It'll be good for the community—and for the students," Larkin's mother had explained, as the three of them sat in what had become their usual spots at the kitchen table. Pal, who had only once tried to climb up onto the fourth chair—"Pal, *no*," Claire had said—was parked in the doorway between the kitchen and the living room, his tail thumping slightly as he watched the conversation.

"I'm fine with it," Claire said. "I mean, you don't think anyone's going to have a problem with us, right?"

"Of course not," Josephine said. "Nearly 20 percent of the Howell student body identifies as queer—that's the term they're using, these days—and this is just one more way of demonstrating our campus's commitment to diversity and inclusion."

"In other words," Larkin had said, "you're doing it for the clout."

"I am doing it because I have come to know a remarkable woman," Josephine said, reaching her hand across the table to meet Claire's, "and I want to show her off."

Now Claire was showing herself in, scraping her boots against the welcome mat and letting Pal pad to his usual spot on the linoleum. "Whoever put that note through the mail slot is long gone, Jo. Nobody casing the joint but me."

"Well, I still don't know what this means," Josephine said, waving towards the note and pulling her hand away before she got close enough to touch it.

"It means that someone thinks you shouldn't be dating Claire," Larkin said, picking up the note and studying its subtext. "Someone's trying to make you feel bad for dating a cop." The four letters had been written in ink, not just once but several times over. A single stroke had not been enough; the writer had written and rewritten until each letter was strong enough to carry the weight of the message. There was a pinhole-sized puncture at the bottom of the second *A*. There was no signature.

"That doesn't make any sense," Josephine said. "We're both women. We're both employed in traditionally male fields. We're bridging the town-gown divide. That's *progressive*." She looked towards the front window again. "I put one of those signs in the yard."

Larkin thought about telling her mother that framing her relationship with Claire in terms of *bridging a town-gown divide* might be nearly as bad as dating a cop, at least in terms of how it would be received on social media. Then she pulled out her phone and started searching for clues. Her first search was for *Josephine Day*, then *Dean Day*, then—although she was pretty sure the note wasn't meant for Claire—*Officer Novak*. When Larkin tried *Howell College dean*, she found something.

"Look at this," Larkin said, turning the screen towards her mother and Claire.

when you think Howell College is a safe space and then your dean brings a cop to Pancake Breakfast

"What's Pancake Breakfast?"

"It's this thing we do on the first day of finals week," Josephine explained. "All the faculty and administrators wear their pajamas and serve pancakes to the students."

There was a second post.

omg they just kissed each other

"I hate Pancake Breakfast," Josephine said. "I wanted to have it canceled, but I was outvoted. They say it makes students feel comfortable."

I have never felt less safe

"I think it made at least one student uncomfortable," Larkin said. The profile photo associated with the account revealed a slick of yellow hair and not much else; the student appeared to be going for some kind of artistic look, and most of their face was hidden. "Do you know who this is?"

Josephine took the phone and studied it carefully, stretching her fingers to expand the image. "No," she finally said, handing the phone back. "Can you find out?"

"Maybe," Larkin said. She kept scrolling.

forgot to mention that the cop-kisser didn't even wear pajamas

"I was dressed appropriately for the event," Larkin's mother said, when Larkin turned the phone around. "I was wearing a Howell sweatshirt."

I sold her that sweatshirt yesterday afternoon

"I couldn't find my other one! I even checked the laundry!"

it cost more than I make in a week

"It cost ninety-two dollars—and yes, I know, *that's expensive*, I've been arguing for years that our campus bookstore is financially inaccessible to at least a third of our student body."

this whole event is a joke

"Whoever this person is, they got that part right," Josephine said. "Pancake Breakfast is one of the most insulting things we do, as a collegiate community."

"Come on, Jo," Claire said. "I thought it was kind of fun."

"Well, sure," Josephine said. "On the surface, it's this fun event. Faculty and staff handing out pancakes to students. And right below the surface—which is to say, the real reason we're doing it—is because it's supposed to represent this dissolving of hierarchies. Your dean, dressed in clothing typically reserved for the intimacy of the home, serving you food! Your professor, who will be grading the exam you're going to complete later this afternoon, asking whether you prefer blueberries or banana slices!"

"You know we do the same thing," Claire said. "Except ours is more of a fundraiser."

"And you don't wear pajamas," Josephine said. "And you actually make your pancakes. Ours are exactly the same as the ones you'd get in the dining hall. Which means that when you really look at what's going on, you see a group of cafeteria workers making the same breakfast they make every morning, for the same pay, only this time they're asked to step out of the way so a bunch of higher-paid academics in mommy-and-daddy drag can transfer pancakes to plates!"

Larkin, who had been scrolling the student's timeline during her mother's anti-Pancake Breakfast screed—"this is why we have a town-and-gown problem in Pratincola!" —discovered one more post that appeared related to both the previous and the current events.

if I bomb this final it's because I had to accept maple syrup from a cop

There was a timestamp on the post, of course. There were timestamps on all of the student's posts—and Larkin stood up, picked the anonymous note off the table, and said "I think I can figure out who did it."

"Really?" her mother said.

"Sure," Larkin said. "Give me 24 hours." She turned to Claire. "Is there any reason this needs to be a legal thing? Like, did this student break any laws that you're aware of?"

"They put a threatening note through my mail slot!" Josephine said.

"Maybe," Claire said, "but I'd argue that the note contains no actual threat."

"They tampered with the federal mail!"

"Actually," Claire said, "they found a loophole. Mail-boxes are federal property. Mail slots are not. So far they're still doing okay, legal-wise."

"Which means I could find out who this person is," Larkin said, "and we wouldn't need to make a big deal out of it."

"Right," Claire said. Larkin liked Claire. She had liked Claire ever since Claire had helped Larkin solve her first murder—and she liked Claire even more now that the square-shouldered, auburn-haired police officer had taken partial residence in her mother's home, bringing one elderly golden retriever, an extremely comprehensive knowledge of how to grill meat, and a perpetually replenishing stack of pulpy paperback novels from the Pratincola public library. The three of them had spent the twelve days of Christmas together, in the living room, reading—and if Claire's book had a flaming sword on the cover and

Josephine's book included the word *Leadership* in the title and Larkin's book was technically a phone, nobody cared.

"Why wouldn't we want to make a big deal out of it?" Josephine said. "I mean, I know why we wouldn't want to make a *big* deal out of it, but are we going to make a small deal? Any deal?"

"No," Larkin and Claire said at the same time.

"Why not?"

"Because police reform is a big issue right now," Larkin said, "and this student probably thought they were being an activist."

"And," Claire said, "because I'm not a bastard."

She put her arm around Josephine's waist. Pal thumped his tail on the floor. Larkin, phone still in hand, sent a quick text to her maybe-sorta boyfriend.

Do you still have that Howell sweatshirt I left at your place

You should probably keep it for a while

Will explain tomorrow, at lunch

Larkin almost sent Ed a heart emoji. Then she deleted it and sent a sandwich emoji instead. That was another problem she needed to solve, tomorrow—or at least *start solving*, since she was pretty sure she wouldn't be able to get this one done in 24 hours. In many ways Larkin envied her mother and Claire, who had found happiness together so quickly—which was one of the reasons why she wanted to restore their happiness as quickly as possible.

"Hey, Mom," Larkin said, pulling up the social-media selfie Bonnie had taken earlier that afternoon. "I did a fitness."

She handed the phone over to her mother, twitching her nose as she did so—their long-established secret signal, which could mean anything from *I love you* to *be careful*. In this case, it meant *everything's going to be okay*.

"Wow," Josephine said, twitching her nose back at Larkin. "You sure look like you did *something*."

"You kind of smell like you did, too," Claire said. "If you don't mind my saying so." She leaned into Josephine's side so she could get a better look at the photo. "Blithe and Bonnie, huh?"

"Was she born on a Sunday?" This was directed at Claire, not at Larkin, and Claire gave Larkin just enough of a glance and a nod to let her know that she understood what Larkin had done—and she approved.

"I'll start the coffee," Larkin said, taking her phone and leaving her mother and her mother's girlfriend to whatever they needed to do now that they'd calmed down. "And then I am *finally* going to go take a shower."

She really was, too—but first she was going to hold the coffee pot under the faucet and pour the water into the coffeemaker and scoop the coffee grounds into the filter and use her free hand to scroll through the pictures that Bonnie had taken, since she hadn't had the chance to look at them yet. All she had been able to tell, before handing the phone to her mother, was that she looked *terrible*.

Bonnie's followers appeared to agree; the photo of Ed and Bonnie had 4,387 likes, and the one of Bonnie and Larkin only had 1,395.

It also had a man, in the background, that Larkin hadn't noticed before. Hadn't noticed at all, really— because he hadn't been in their guided fitness class. She was sure of it. First clue, he wasn't wearing anything you'd want to work out in. He had the kind of jacket that was made up entirely of pockets, unzipped to reveal a sweater over a collared shirt. His sweater looked new; his jeans looked a decade old. Second clue, he appeared only in Larkin's photo. By the time Bonnie had taken the picture with Ed, the mysterious figure was gone.

Larkin would have written him off as somebody's husband or boyfriend or partner, except she didn't recognize him—not exactly, anyway. As Larkin expanded the photo to get a closer look at the man's glasses and freckles and graying ginger hair, Larkin suddenly realized she'd seen him before.

Many times, in fact.

She just couldn't remember where.

CHAPTER 4

"Do you recognize this person?" Larkin turned her phone towards Ed. She had already expanded the image, revealing the man with the ginger hair and obscuring the woman with the red, sweaty face. Not that Larkin minded Ed seeing her all sweaty, not necessarily; if anything, it was a demonstration of her commitment to her Future Self. If Larkin took that fitness class as often as Bonnie taught it, she would eventually be as lithe as her instructor—or, at least, in better shape than she was at present. That was what education promised, after all; and if Larkin knew that only a small percentage of her former students would ever find careers as actors, it didn't stop her from hoping that she would be the one person in Bonnie's fitness class who actually got fit.

"Sorry," Ed said, returning the phone and taking another bite of his sandwich. The two of them were in The Coffee Shop—and Larkin had lived in Pratincola for nearly three months before she realized that was the business's *actual name*—sharing a quick lunch at the end of

Larkin's shift. Larkin worked from 6 a.m. to 1 p.m. most days, a seven-hour shift that entitled her to a fifteen-minute break and a 20 percent discount on any food or drink she bought for herself. Larkin's boss had started letting her ring up the discount code for Ed, too, since they ate lunch together so often. Her boss liked Ed.

"I thought you might know him," Larkin said, closing out her photo app and opening her social media feed. "Since you know everybody."

"Since everybody knows me," Ed corrected, smiling. He had been well known in the Eastern Iowa Creative Corridor—the stretch of towns, colleges, startups, and corporate hubs that connected Cedar Rapids and Iowa City—even before he had taken his unexpected walk onto the stage during the last movement of Beethoven's Ninth Symphony. His role in saving that performance had already eclipsed Larkin's role in solving the murder that had taken place during rehearsals, probably because Ed's last-minute tenor solo had gone viral on social media and Larkin's name hadn't even been included in the police report.

But that was fine—it had to be fine—because Ed was still sitting across the table from her and not spending time with any of the other women who cooed and aahed over CR's Newest Star. Larkin watched their faces every time she and Ed walked into a room together, eyes shifting from admiration to confusion, from desire to disappointment.

Now Larkin hid her own disappointment and slid her phone back over the table. "What about this person?"

It was the student who had posted about Pancake Breakfast.

"Oh, sure," Ed said. "That's Ghoti."

"Fish?"

"G-h-o-t-i," Ed said. "George Bernard Shaw's preferred spelling."

Larkin was pretty sure it hadn't been Shaw who had originally posited that the English language was flexible enough to allow *fish* to swim through the phonemes *gh* (as in *tough*), *o* (as in *women*), and *ti* (as in *caution*), but she wasn't interested in arguing the attribution. "How do you know Ghoti?" she asked, hoping Ed wouldn't notice that the conversation was turning into an investigation.

"I had them in Group Voice," Ed said.

"Wait, are you a guided vocal fitness instructor?"

"Yeah," Ed said. "That must be why Bonnie is trying to be my new social media best friend."

Larkin decided to leave that alone, at least for now. "So Ghoti is a vocal student?"

"Nope. We have a class for non-majors, mostly kids who want to sing in the choir, and a class for instrumentalists." He took a sip of the sparkling beverage Larkin had not only recommended but also helped to invent; when she began working at The Coffee Shop, she had made a joke about wanting to serve a *Rosa Pratin-Cola*, after the state flower that had given the town its name, and now she mixed up a batch of rose-flavored soda at the beginning of every shift. "Most high school music teachers have to do band and choir, these days, so we teach the band kids how to sing and the voice kids how to play instruments."

"I bet the group instrumental class is terrible," Larkin said.

"It's not that bad," Ed said. "But it's a lot of work, for the students. They come to Howell thinking music is all about feelings, and we start teaching theory and showing them how to prepare a double reed, and about a third of them drop." He winked at Larkin. "A lot of them transfer to theater."

"Of course," Larkin said. "Because theater involves *no work at all.*"

"Well," Ed said, "your department has a lot more *rolling around on the floor pretending to be bacon.*"

Larkin did not want to remind Ed that theater was no longer her department. Instead, she showed him Ghoti's latest social media rant, handing over her phone so he could wipe his fingers on his napkin and begin to scroll.

"Today I learned about alternative learning preferences," Ed read aloud. "For example, in this class I may prefer to submit a collage of images instead of writing an essay."

"That's way worse than pretending to be bacon," Larkin said. "Come on, come on, come on, *you know it's worse.*"

"Shhhh," Ed said. "I'm reading."

welcome to college here's your gloo stick, Ghoti had written, followed by *wait this professor just said it can be physical or virtual, they don't want anyone to feel burdened by the obligation to buy posterboard,* then *at Howell College posterboard is a burden but tuition is fineeeeeeee,* ending the thread with *I am going to copy five images to a doc instead of writing an essay, it is my learning preference* and *welcome to college here's your right click.*

"Do you let students turn in collages instead of essays?" Larkin asked.

"No," Ed said. "That's one of the good things about being a voice coach; there are no alternatives to learning the music." His sandwich included some kind of squash mélange; he poked a bit of butternut back between the house-baked bread. "The notes are either right or they aren't."

"Right," Larkin said. Her sandwich had included peanut butter and house-mashed rhubarb jam; she'd jammed most of it down while Ed was tending to his herbal tea, leaving just enough of the sandwich on her plate to pretend that she was still in the process of eating it. "And if they aren't, you can help the student make adjustments."

"To an extent," Ed said. "I assume you got the same instructions I did—never touch the students, never ask them to place their hands on your body or any other student's body, always make sure there's a third party in the room whenever you do one-on-one coaching."

"I was told to always have an assistant director or assistant stage manager in the room with me," Larkin said, "but it's hard to do theater without touching people."

"It's hard to do music without touching people!" Ed said. "Pun intended." He looked at his sandwich, then at the novelty clock that had been mounted to the right of The Coffee Shop's door. It was currently *time for coffee* until *time for coffee*, or 25 minutes to 1. "But it also required us to get more specific about what we did, you know. It wasn't necessarily a bad thing. We've learned how to talk to students about activating their diaphragms without falling back on, like, *put your hand here.*"

"We couldn't say diaphragm," Larkin said. "We had to say *core.*"

"And if making those changes help to prevent some of the abuses of power that we both know were endemic to the art world," Ed said, "maybe they're worth it."

"Maybe," Larkin said. She thought of the abuses of power she and Ed and Anni had uncovered, when the three of them had gotten themselves inadvertently involved with the death of Harrison Tucker. Although the murder had taken place in the *town* half of Pratincola, the case had been, at its core, an academic dispute. "Or maybe people have just found different ways of manipulating each other." She ate the last bite of her sandwich, since it was clear that Ed was about to clear their table. "If I were going to actually finish my dissertation, I'd want to start all over so I could write it on *that*—the idea that there are always going to be people with competing objectives, and if they can't achieve their objectives with Tactic A, they are required *by the rules of drama* to pursue Tactic B, and then C, and so on, until they're either married or dead."

"Married or dead," Ed said. "Good title." He stacked Larkin's plate on top of his; she looped three fingers around two mug handles, freeing her other hand to squeeze Ed's shoulder and kiss his cheek. "I'd write it right now," she said, "but I have to get back to work—and then I have to get over to the campus bookshop to interrogate Ghoti."

"Wait," Ed said. "Why? What's going on?"

Larkin considered the conflict that could arise if she asked Ed what he thought about the phrase *all cops are bastards*. Then she identified her objective and chose her tactic. "Ghoti called Mom out on social media," Larkin said, "and Mom wants to know how to make it right. You know, *doing best by the student body* kind of thing."

"Best of luck," Ed said. Then he placed their plates neatly in the bus tub and planted a very quick kiss on Larkin's lips. She could tell, by the crinkles at the edges of his eyes and the way the corners of his mouth touched hers, that he was happy to do it; there was no hesitancy in his action and no anxiety about how his kiss would be received.

She could not tell a single additional thing about the state of their relationship.

Larkin made it to the Howell bookstore five minutes before Ghoti's shift should have ended; she had successfully assessed the student's schedule from their social media posts, but had failed to account for the time between *off the clock* and *off the job.*

"Ghoti is still doing inventory," the manager had said, barely looking up from the point-of-sale system. "They'll be out when they're done."

While Larkin waited, she wandered through the various displays—sweatshirts, textbooks, cling-film decals that could be placed on phones and laptops and cars—confirming that both her mother and Ghoti had been correct: there was very little in this bookstore that could be considered *affordable,* even if it were the parent making the purchase instead of the student. The sweatshirt that Josephine had bought to replace the one that Larkin had misplaced at Ed's apartment did in fact cost $92; the hoodie version cost $125. A Howell-branded hydroflask was $49.95. A Howell-branded bumper sticker was $15. Larkin didn't even bother walking through the part of the bookstore that sold books; she already knew, from experience, how much people charged for academic texts—and how long it would take her to pay off the portion of her loans that she might have avoided by borrowing copies of Stanislavsky and *Hedda Gabler* from the library. *But you'll need this,* she had thought to herself—the same as everybody thinks, whether they're paying textbook prices for a collection of public-domain plays or buying a mass-produced pajama top embroidered with the words "Proud Howell Mom." *You'll want this. It's part of who you are.*

Now Larkin was someone entirely different—or, at

least, different enough to wish she had made fewer purchases.

Ghoti, when they finally appeared, was also *different*. Larkin could see that as soon as she spotted the lank yellow hair hanging over the reddened, pimpled face. It wasn't that Ghoti appeared uninterested in either the beauty standard or the gender binary, since Larkin had met many students who refused to categorize themselves within those sociocultural boundaries—but those students had chosen to be compelling on their own merits, and had cultivated physical presentations that correlated with their sense of self.

Ghoti's self, on the other hand, was centered on *right-eousness*—and Larkin followed, half-hidden behind a display of Valentine's Day cards, as Ghoti began sliding their fingers over a grease-streaked phone.

The slithy tove made me work sixteen minutes without pay

Got corkscrewed out of one dollar and ninety-three cents

I learned that math before I came to college btw

My college math class is a computer program that gets mad if I read too quickly

There is a timer in the corner of the screen

If you try to move on before the timer runs out, it tells you that learning requires time and attention

Larkin wanted to let Ghoti continue, to see what else she could learn by paying attention—but she was running out of time. "Hey," she said, approaching the reproachful figure. "Can I talk to you for a minute?"

Ghoti stopped swiping their screen and swiped one lock of hair away from a pair of irritated eyes. "I don't know, *can you*?"

Game met game. "Well played," Larkin said, watching Ghoti register the compliment as a gesture of mutual respect. "Now that we know the answer, I need to ask you a question."

The respect disappeared. "Do you need to," Ghoti said, "or do you want to?"

"Are you an English major?"

"Is that the question?"

"No," Larkin said. The planes of Ghoti's face slid between the planks of their hair. Larkin asked herself *what Ghoti wanted*. Then she changed her tactic.

"I saw what you posted online."

"That is literally the whole point of posting online," Ghoti said, turning their attention back to their phone. "So other people will see it."

This tactic was going nowhere, and Ghoti was getting away—so Larkin tried again. "You were right."

This time Ghoti pushed enough hair behind one ear to both see and listen. "About what?"

"So far," Larkin said, "nearly everything."

Ghoti almost smiled; then they matched their face to Larkin's modifier. "So this is the part where you tell me I was wrong about something."

"Right again," Larkin said. "But I was going to ask you a question first." This was not the same question Larkin had originally planned to ask, but Ghoti didn't need to know that. "Do you know who I am?"

Larkin watched Ghoti evaluate potential options, their eyebrows contracting before relaxing into recognition. "You're Dr. Jackson's girlfriend."

"Yes," Larkin said, wondering if Ghoti had known to use that word because Ed had used it first, although he didn't seem like the type of professor who brought his personal life into a group voice lesson. "And I'm Dean Day's daughter. And"—because she needed to stop the look of disgust that was twisting into the left half of Ghoti's blotchy cheek—"I'm a private detective."

"Wow," Ghoti said, brushing the remaining hair out of their face and looking at Larkin with their first glimmer of genuine interest—and Larkin realized that she had been wrong about what Ghoti wanted. It wasn't that Ghoti was hoping that someone would read their social media posts. It wasn't even that Ghoti wanted someone to tell them that they were right about everything. It was, simply, that Ghoti wanted to be an adult—and they were stuck in a situation where everyone treated them like a child.

"So I came to tell you that Officer Claire Novak *is not a bastard*," Larkin said.

"Aren't all cops bastards?" Ghoti asked, the smile they had previously disallowed beginning to reform.

"Not this one," Larkin said. "That proves the entire statement wrong."

"Not according to Aristotle," Ghoti said. "The statement *all cops are bastards* includes both *some cops are bastards* and *no cops are not bastards*. You have to prove both premises are false before you can pass judgment on the entire deduction."

Larkin had planned to base *her* argument on ethics; now that she understood how Ghoti might respond to that kind of philosophical dialogue, she switched to semantics. "I've been to Claire's house. Seen the family photos on the refrigerator. Third kid out of four."

"Other three are boys," Ghoti said.

"Of course they are," Larkin said, rewarding Ghoti's correct guess with a grin of her own. "And her parents, *whom I've met*, have been married for as long as she's been alive. Officer Novak is one cop who is as legitimate as they come, and I would appreciate you treating her that way."

CHAPTER 5

"And so this student said they'd stop being a jerk to Mom and Claire," Larkin said, telling the story to Anni the same way she'd told it to her mother and Claire the night before. "Except now I'm pretty sure I have to open that detective agency. Otherwise Ghoti is going to find out and drag me on social media."

"Did you start working on your business plan?" Anni asked, leaning her canvas bag against the fitness classroom wall and taking a preemptive sip from her water bottle.

"No," Larkin said, bending over in an attempt to get in some of what she considered *stretching* before they had to do what Bonnie considered *stretching*, which stretched the definition of the word to its limit—which, to be fair, was kind of Bonnie's brand. "I was busy solving an actual mystery. Like a real detective!"

"A real detective registers their business with the State of Iowa," Anni said.

Larkin's head was close enough to her toes for her to pretend she hadn't heard that. "And it wasn't even a murder! See? I can solve anything, just like you said."

bag, and Larkin knew it had something to do with the message Anni had just sent; even an amateur detective could figure out that Anni had made some kind of plan with some other person.

"Right," Larkin said. "Not tonight. Fine."

"We can still walk back together," Anni said. "That's a good five-minute planning session."

"I'm going to walk the track," Larkin said. "Since it's apparently the one piece of fitness equipment in the entire building that *actually works*."

She left without saying goodbye to Anni or Ed, although she didn't realize that until her second lap. It took another lap around the track for Larkin to realize that it wasn't sweat trickling from her eyes. She paused, lifted up the oversized T-shirt she had borrowed from her mother, and blew her nose into the bottom.

"Keep moving or get out of the way," somebody said. Larkin tried the first option for another half a lap, then switched to the second. She'd go to her locker, get her mother's coat, walk back to The Coffee Shop, text Anni to set up their next business planning session, text Ed to set up the whole *we-need-to-talk* thing, and drive back home.

It was a plan. Larkin Day was neither a detective nor a girlfriend, but she could still put together a plan.

She got as far as the locker room.

"Larkin!" Bonnie said, sitting on the bench as if she had been waiting for her to arrive. Larkin didn't know Bonnie used the locker rooms. She didn't know Bonnie *sat*. She did know that Bonnie had been crying—much harder than Larkin had been, and for a much longer period of time. Larkin thought about offering Bonnie her mother's shirt, and then decided to offer Bonnie a wad of paper towels instead.

"I need to hire you," Bonnie said, taking the towels and

twisting them between her hands. "I've just been murdered."

CHAPTER 6

arkin sat in the passenger side of Bonnie's cherry-red SUV, unzipping her mother's coat as Bonnie started the engine. "Do you mind if I record this?" Larkin knew, from her last murder mystery, that Iowa was one of the 38 states in which it was legal to record people without their consent. However, she still wanted to ask—especially because she wanted to ask Bonnie *a lot of questions.*

Bonnie nodded. "Is this for the podcast?"

"No," Larkin said. "It's for the investigation." She wasn't quite sure about the legality of conducting an investigation without the accompanying paperwork, but she'd figure all of that out later. First, she had to figure out why a person who was *obviously still alive* was insisting that she had been murdered.

"All right," Larkin said. "Tell me what happened."

"Well," Bonnie began—and then she glanced at Larkin's phone, which sat between them on the center console. "Do you want me to say it in a specific way? Like, should I introduce myself first, so your audience will know who I am?"

"There's no audience," Larkin said. "Just me."

"But you might want to use this later," Bonnie said. "Maybe for your website or something. Or—you know, we should do video, because then we'll have both, and you can always strip the audio out later, and—"

This was the first time Larkin had investigated someone who was not only actively aware that she was being investigated, but also actively wanted to direct the process. Luckily, there was only one process that mattered —and it was a process developed in 1936 by actor and director Konstantin Stanislavsky. Before Larkin could ask any of the questions that could help her solve the case, she had to ask herself *what Bonnie wanted.*

"From the top, then." Larkin put a bit more of her theater training into her voice, deepening her timbre until she sounded like her mother's favorite public radio personality. "Bonnie Cooper, can you tell us why you think you've been murdered?"

"I don't think I've been murdered," Bonnie said, pitching her voice a bit higher than the one she typically used. "I know I have." Bonnie held out her phone, tapping it until the screen turned white. "Take a look."

"It's a login screen."

Bonnie shook her head. "You have to tell them what you're looking at."

"Bonnie showed me her phone," Larkin said. "It showed a login screen." Bonnie shook her head again. "Sorry, I can do better." Larkin cleared her throat. "Bonnie Cooper handed me her phone." She held out her hand; Bonnie, without hesitation, obliged. "It was pink, of course, to match her headset and her athletic shoes. Very clean. The protective cover appeared to have been provided by one of her sponsors."

"That's right," Bonnie said. "Last November I signed a contract with Drink, which is one of the fastest-growing nutrition-hydration solutions on the market."

"Is it a drink?"

"They love it when you ask that," Bonnie said. "It's literally a *solution*. There's science involved. I can't say how much money Drink offered me, of course, but it was life-changing."

"You might say, then," said Larkin, "that Drink was the solution to some of your financial problems?"

"No," Bonnie said. "We need to redo that. First of all, we can't say that Drink solves anything. That was very clear in their marketing package. Second of all, I don't want to imply that I had financial problems. Because I didn't. And even if I did, you always need to come at your audience from a point of strength. You want them to *want to be you*. That's the only way any of this works."

"Okay," Larkin said. She handed Bonnie her phone. Then she took her own phone and turned off the recording app. "This is not working."

"Why not?"

"Because it's completely fake, okay?" Larkin stowed her phone in the depths of her mother's coat. "First of all, I don't have a podcast. Second of all, you don't sound like you're coming from a position of strength. You sound like someone who is contractually obligated to get excited about nutritional goo."

"It's not a goo."

"I don't care *what it isn't*," Larkin asked. "What matters is *what you are*. None of this is real, Bonnie, and the people who follow you recognize that, because *none of them want to be you.* They either want to fuck you, or they're your family, or they want you to fail."

"That's not true," Bonnie said, her voice still pitched towards the podcast they were no longer recording. "I have *fans*. My subscribers are in the *five figures*."

Larkin ignored this. "Third of all," she continued, "you haven't been murdered."

"Yes," Bonnie said, and this time she used her real voice—firm, calm, flat-voweled. "I have."

She tapped her phone screen until it glowed.

"Look," she said. "My phone doesn't know who I am anymore."

Bonnie held the phone in front of her face. She rubbed her fingers over the appropriate sensors. Then she pulled down on the screen and swiped a numeric password. "It won't let me in," she said, turning the phone towards Larkin. "See?"

"So you've been hacked," Larkin said.

"I've been murdered," Bonnie said. "Everywhere. Try to find me online."

Larkin had to pull the bottom corner of her mother's coat onto her lap before she could reach the part of the pocket where her phone had fallen. Then she began searching—first Bonnie's name, which only revealed that there were hundreds of other people named Bonnie Cooper, then Bonnie's social media accounts.

"You post under *Blithe and Bonnie*, right?" Larkin said. She went into her history and tried to access the photo of Ed that Bonnie had taken two days ago. *Page not found.* She did an advanced search on *@blitheandbonnie*, turning up one dead link after another. She even went to the Internet Archive and tried to access previously stored images of Bonnie's social media accounts—but the Wayback

Machine had no record of anything Bonnie had ever posted, published, or shared.

"You've been completely erased," Larkin said. "Not just the accounts. The content, too. Even the archives."

"And my email," Bonnie said. "And anything I've ever put on the cloud. I'm not even sure my phone number still works. Can you try to text me?"

Larkin didn't have Bonnie's number stored into her phone; she had to take dictation before sending Bonnie a two-word text. The two of them waited; the message never arrived.

"All right," Larkin said. "You've been murdered. Sort of."

"About as murdered as you can be without being dead."

Larkin considered this. Without an online presence, without *online access*, a person like Bonnie could effectively argue that they no longer existed—even if they were very much alive. "All right," she said again. "We'll call it a murder."

"Can you figure out who did it?"

"I don't know," Larkin said. "First I need to figure out how this could have happened." This was the kind of case that would require the kind of person who knew all of the internet rules—how email accounts worked, how a person could lose access to their social media, all of the ways in which the Wayback Machine might have deleted Bonnie's archives—and the one person Larkin knew who could either provide or access that information just happened to have recently volunteered to serve as her pro bono assistant.

Larkin quickly texted Anni—*important murder business can we talk*—and asked Bonnie if she could drive them both over to the building that housed both The Coffee Shop and

Anni's apartment. Anni responded to Larkin's text —*coming right down*—as Bonnie pulled her SUV into The Coffee Shop's parking lot.

"You know Anni Morgan, right?" Larkin asked.

"Yes," Bonnie said. "Pixie cut. Glasses. See, there she is—"

Bonnie pointed at Anni, who had exited the building's double glass doors without looking for Larkin. Instead, Anni walked quickly to the curb, looked both ways, crossed the street, and—Larkin had to twist her entire body around to see—opened the driver-side door of a parked car.

"Wait," Larkin said. "Anni doesn't drive."

The car backed up, signaled, and pulled away.

"And she definitely doesn't drive a car with Illinois plates," Larkin said. She turned to Bonnie. "I can't believe I'm saying this," she said, "but *follow that car.*"

CHAPTER 7

I t was unsurprisingly easy to tail Anni; she drove just under the speed limit, and signaled her upcoming turns half-a-block in advance. This gave Larkin plenty of opportunity to read the multiple bumper stickers carefully arranged across the back end of the vehicle— although *read*, in this case, was a relative term. Many of the bumper stickers featured strings of letters and numbers interrupted by brackets and parentheses. The sticker placed on the top left displayed an array of playing cards; the one on the bottom right read "your card is the ace of spades" and Larkin had to admit that it *was*, though she couldn't have said *how*.

"Why are we doing this?" Bonnie asked.

Larkin couldn't answer that question either—or at least not in a way that Bonnie would have found relevant to her murder investigation. "Because Anni *doesn't drive*," she said again, and both Anni and Bonnie kept driving.

They passed the Pratincola Fitness Complex, bright and inviting against the five-o'-clock darkness, before getting separated by a yellow light; the car with the Illinois plates made it through, making a careful and precise left turn before signaling its intent to ascend the ramp towards I-380. "Are we following them onto the highway?" Bonnie asked, the two of them stalled under the red glow of the intersection.

"I don't know," Larkin said. "I mean, *yes*. Right? Didn't you think something was wrong?"

"I don't know anything about Anni," Bonnie began, "but—"

"How can you not know anything about her?" Larkin said. "Anni's been taking your class longer than I have! She's the one who's always helping all of the new students, which means she is literally *doing your job*."

The light changed; Bonnie flipped her turn signal to the right and twisted her steering wheel towards downtown Pratincola.

"All right," Bonnie said. "So the deal with my class— sorry, I'm just going to take us back to your car—is that every section I teach needs to match every other section taught by every other licensed instructor. Like, *around the world*."

They were passing the fitness complex again. "Which means that I have a script. It comes through my headset, and I'm not supposed to add anything to it. None of my own words. Because if I say something off-script and it, like, *goes viral*, it could make the entire company look bad."

"What if it makes the company look good? What if it's, like, a fitness instructor who stops the music to help a struggling student figure out what a burpee is?"

"We can't stop the music," Bonnie said. "We advertise these classes based on the number of calories you could burn in each session and the amount of muscle you could build over the course of a year, and those numbers only work if we stick to the plan." They were back at Anni's apartment building. "I mean, most students don't hit those numbers because maybe they don't attend every class or they don't put their full effort into every session, but those numbers have to be a legal possibility."

She turned off the car and turned to Larkin. "Which is why not being able to access my phone is a huge deal. The company is going to know that I didn't complete my class. I'm going to get a demerit, and I'm not going to be able to explain it because I can't get in touch with them."

"You could call them," Larkin said. "You could use my phone."

"They don't do phone calls," Bonnie said. "There's just this online dashboard, and your login is one of three approved social media platforms, which means I am locked out. For all intensive purposes"—Larkin thought about correcting her, and then thought better of it—"I am dead to them."

Bonnie pushed a button on the driver's side door; Larkin heard her own door unlock. "Can you solve my murder by Friday? Otherwise, I'll miss another class and get another demerit. Which isn't the worst thing that can happen to you, there are ways to get un-demerited, but most of them involve bringing a certain number of new members to the platform, and I can't do that if I'm murdered."

"Wait," Larkin said. "Is this a fitness pyramid scheme?"

"No," Bonnie said. "You sound like my dad. It's a real job." She sighed. "I don't want to lose this. I don't want to lose my class, I don't want to lose Drink—they're my first real sponsor, really—and I don't want to lose my followers, and I just started making enough money that I maybe don't have to get help from my parents anymore." She tapped at her phone again, waved it in front of her face, powered it down. "Can you help me?"

"I'll try," Larkin said. "But it would go a lot faster if we had Anni's help."

"Which means she would be doing *your* job?" Bonnie said, smiling, and for the first time Larkin saw the person Bonnie Cooper could be if she didn't have to be a literal mouthpiece for fitness companies and nutrition solutions. She liked this person a lot better than the persona Bonnie presented in class and on social media—and it made Larkin wonder, just for a moment, whether solving Bonnie's murder was actually a good idea.

Of course, that's what she'd thought about her last murder. If Anni were there, she would tell Larkin that real detectives, in addition to registering their businesses with the State of Iowa, did not continuously ask themselves whether they *really needed to solve the cases that came their way*. But Anni was not in the car with them. She was in someone else's car—and that was a mystery that Larkin *really, really needed to solve*, especially if she was going to have any chance of solving this one.

"I'm going to text Anni," Larkin said, unbuckling her seatbelt and opening the car door just enough to smell the ice-cold Iowa evening. The January air pulled the moisture out of her nose, sending it on a slow journey towards her upper lip. *"Where are you,"* Larkin said, showing the message to Bonnie before sending it.

"Lucky you," Bonnie said. "Still being able to text." Her real smile—which Larkin noticed for the second time —was slightly asymmetrical. "Never thought I'd say that."

"Never thought I'd be asked to solve the murder of someone who isn't actually dead," Larkin said. She set her text notifications to vibrate, to ensure she didn't miss Anni's response.

And she didn't—but that was because it never arrived.

———

"Do you think I should have followed her?" Larkin asked her mother, after she had taken her shower and taken the leftovers out of the refrigerator. That night they were having Claire's famous chili (secret ingredient: ancho pepper), Larkin's not-so-famous guacamole (secret ingredient: brown sugar), and the cornbread muffins Josephine had made from a Famous Savings mix (secret ingredients: water, egg).

"Are you asking me as your mother, or are you asking me as the mother of Pratincola's best private detective?" Larkin watched as Josephine carefully sliced her muffin in half, putting the two largest pieces on her plate and transferring the crumbles to the top of her chili bowl.

"I don't know," Larkin said. She held her muffin over her bowl, poked it with her thumb, and watched the cornbrittles fall. "I guess both."

"Well," Larkin's mother said, "Anni is your friend."

"And you shouldn't stalk your friends," Larkin said, making a fist around the rest of her cornbread muffin. "Even when they're driving away in someone else's car."

"Do you think Anni stole the car?"

"Of course not." Larkin said. "Anni doesn't steal things. The last time we were at The Coffee Shop, she accidentally took, like, five napkins out of the napkin dispenser—which was probably my fault, since I was the one who loaded that napkin dispenser—and she put the extra napkins on the top of the dispenser for the next person to use."

"Well—"

"And then she took a sticky note out of her bag,

because she always has everything in her bag, and she wrote *these napkins are clean* on the sticky note."

"Well—"

"And then I told her that the napkin she touched with the sticky note was probably no longer clean, and she got all flustered, you know, like she does, and I said I would use that napkin. Even though it had her sticky note on it."

"Well—"

"And then I ended up using all the napkins anyway, because I made my peanut butter sandwich with a little extra peanut butter on it. Employee perk."

"So you're pretty sure she didn't steal the car."

"As your daughter and as Pratincola's best unlicensed private detective," Larkin said, "I'm absolutely sure." She opened her fist and let her smushed muffin drop into her chili. "So I probably shouldn't have followed her."

"You probably shouldn't have," Josephine said. She put a dollop of guacamole on the side of her plate, then used a butter knife to spread a portion of guac onto a bite-sized piece of cornbread. "So why did you?"

"Because Anni doesn't drive, and she doesn't drive a car with Illinois plates, and she doesn't text me that she's coming right down and then, like, get in a car with someone else."

"Is that the real problem?" Josephine asked. "That Anni is spending time with someone who isn't you?"

"No," Larkin said, using the back of her spoon to submerge her mushed-up muffin into Claire's famous chili. "I mean—she's just acting all weird, you know? Canceling meetings. Disappearing. *Driving*."

"Have you asked her about any of this?"

"No," Larkin said again. "I wouldn't know what to say."

"That doesn't sound like my daughter," Josephine said.

"Nor does it sound like Pratincola's best soon-to-be-licensed private detective."

Then Larkin's phone vibrated. Three crumbs fell off the bite of cornbread Josephine was attempting to guacamole-butter. Larkin grabbed the phone off the table, swiped at its screen, read the message. *Important murder business?*

Larkin had almost forgotten about the murder.

Her phone vibrated again, with Anni's second text: *Want to talk tomorrow?*

Yes, Larkin texted back. This meant she had two *we-need-to-talk* conversations in her future, neither of which she felt ready to handle. How do you ask your best friend if she's still your best friend, and then ask your boyfriend if he's still your boyfriend? Why was she even having to ask these questions, at thirty-five and three-quarters years old? There had to be a better way of doing all of this—and she had about twelve hours to figure out what it was.

"Can I ask you a question, like, as a dean?"

"Do you mean you want me to answer the question as if I were a dean?" Josephine corrected, twitching her nose at Larkin.

Larkin twitched her nose back, mostly because she knew she was supposed to, and then she took a bite of the mess she had made out of Claire's amazing chili and her mother's less-than-amazing cornbread. "How do you have, like, a difficult conversation with somebody?"

"It's actually not that hard," Josephine said. "You decide what you want to say, you stick to what needs to be said, and you say it."

"And then what?"

Larkin watched her mother smile. "You already know the answer." It wasn't quite her real smile; it was her dean smile, mixed with a bit of her mother smile. "Then you listen."

———

"It was probably someone who had access to her phone," Anni said, the two of them sitting in their usual places in Anni's studio apartment—which meant that Larkin had the sofa and Anni had the desk chair; the piano bench; the portion of the coffee table not occupied by mugs, coasters, or potted plants; the portion of the sofa not occupied by Larkin; and all of the pacing it took to get from one station to another. Every time she sat on the coffee table, she took a sip of her tea.

"So it could be someone she lives with," Larkin said.

"Or a boyfriend," Anni said. "Or a girlfriend. Or a thief."

Anni's face reddened slightly, and Larkin suddenly wondered if her friend's unusual behavior had anything to do with *boyfriends or girlfriends*. That made even less sense than the driving thing; Anni had told Larkin, when they first met, that she was uninterested in any kind of romantic entanglement. "No double likes," Anni had said, and Larkin had no reason not to believe her. Anni didn't drink anything stronger than herbal tea, didn't eat anything stronger than spinach, practiced her digital piano for an hour every morning, and went to bed at 10 p.m. She was not the kind of person who would enjoy *dating*—and she wasn't really the kind of person other people would enjoy dating. Anni Morgan was nobody's right-swipe.

Which left a single possibility.

Maybe the car really was stolen.

"We can rule out thief," Larkin said, mostly to see how Anni reacted. "Bonnie still has her phone."

"They wouldn't have needed to take it permanently," Anni said, turning to a new page in her notebook and beginning another circuit of the room. "They could have just taken Bonnie's phone for a little while. Long enough to"—she consulted a previous page—"deactivate and potentially delete Bonnie's social media accounts, submit a wipe request to the Internet Archive, confirm the wipe was complete, and then deactivate and potentially delete her email and cloud accounts."

She sipped her tea again. "Maybe not in that order, but close enough."

"Could they have done this without her phone?"

Anni paused, from her perch on the coffee table, to examine the prickles of a pink cactus. "It would have been a lot harder." She stood up again. "You'll have to ask Bonnie to confirm, but I bet she's got auto-login set up on all of her accounts. If you can unlock her phone, you can access any of her apps without having to log in again. No passwords, no two-factor authentication. That's how I'd do it."

The last time Anni had said *that's how I'd do it*, it had turned out to be exactly how the murderer had done it. "How would you unlock her phone, though? You'd need, like, *her face*."

"Or her fingerprint," Anni said. "Or her backup password. Which of those do you think is the easiest to get?"

"Well, Bonnie still has all her fingers," Larkin said. "So someone must have figured out her password."

"Right," Anni said. "And you need to figure out whom."

"Whom-done-it," Larkin said. "I'll get on it as soon as I finish my shift." She stood up—for the first time since they had begun their meeting—and put her coffee mug in the sink. Larkin had about five minutes before she needed to clock in downstairs—which meant it was time for the difficult part of the conversation.

Decide what you want to say. "Hey, can I ask—is something going on?"

"What do you mean?"

Stick to what needs to be said. "I don't know, you've just been extra busy lately."

"I don't think that's true," Anni said. "I'm actually very careful to *never let myself get busy.* Time pressure is how you make mistakes."

"Well," Larkin said, "you did make a mistake. You texted me yesterday that you were coming right down and then you didn't."

"What?" Anni said. "When did I—"

Larkin held out her phone screen. "Oh," Anni said, picking up her plant mister and aiming the spray at her three-foot-high rubber plant. "That text wasn't for you. I'm sorry. I hope you weren't waiting for me."

"Who was it for?"

"I'm sorry?" This time she didn't sound sorry at all.

"Who were you texting?"

"I… um…" Anni never lied. Instead, she set the plant mister down on her digital piano. Then she picked it up again, placed the mister on one of her coffee-table coasters, and carefully wiped away the residue of its temporary displacement. "I think you're going to be late to work."

Larkin picked up the plant mister; she'd been in the apartment often enough to know that it belonged on the windowsill, next to the jade plant and the leggy succulent Anni lovingly called her *etiolated echeveria.* "Just leave that there," Anni said, and Larkin put it down again. "You should take the stairs, just in case the elevator is slow."

"Yeah, okay," Larkin said. Anni was probably right— again—but Larkin wasn't sure where she'd gone wrong. Had she forgotten to *listen*? "See you tomorrow, maybe?

I'll get in touch with Bonnie this evening and let you know who might have had access to her phone."

"Sure," Anni said, picking up her plant mister and putting it where Larkin hadn't. "You'd better *run*."

Larkin did run, her feet automatically picking up the pace she'd learned in Bonnie's class—and as she exited the ground-floor stairwell into the lobby, she saw a man waiting for the elevator. The same man she had seen in the background of the photo Bonnie had taken, although she couldn't confirm it because the image had been murdered along with the rest of Bonnie's content—but there he was, a black watch cap pulled over his ginger hair, one hand shoved into the side pocket of his many-zippered jacket, the other hand tapping rhythmically against his phone.

He looked at Larkin, disheveled and breathing heavily from her five-flight dash. She looked back. She was sure she knew him from somewhere—like, years ago, when she was in Los Angeles. Or New York. Or London. She was about to ask him something, to see if he responded in a British accent, when both the elevator and the coffee shop doors opened.

"Larkin!" her boss called—and when he heard her name, the mysterious ginger-haired man nodded, just once, as if he knew her too.

CHAPTER 8

"Who do you think could have had access to your phone?" Larkin sat across the table from Bonnie, who had agreed to meet Larkin at The Coffee Shop as soon as Larkin's shift was over. Getting in touch with Bonnie had proved to be a challenge, since phone calls, emails, and texting were no longer options; in the end Larkin had called the fitness center directly and asked them if it was possible to leave Bonnie a message. The young woman on the other end of the phone had agreed to put a note in Bonnie's cubby, which was kindergarten-level technology at best—but the message had been received, and now Bonnie passed a bottle of sparkling water from hand to hand and tried to answer Larkin's question.

"All kinds of people, I guess." Bonnie was still wearing her workout clothes: pink sports bra, pink-and-black leggings, and a midriff-baring hoodie that bore the Drink logo. "I do the same thing everyone else does, right? You put your phone in your bag and you put your bag up against the wall, and you tell yourself nobody will touch your stuff because it's Iowa."

Larkin had done exactly that, once she saw that everyone else in Pratincola was doing it. "So you never put your phone in your locker or anything."

"Of course not." Bonnie picked at the label on her bottle of water, peeling off a nutritional chart similar to the one that ran down the left side of her Drink-branded hoodie. The bottled water had fewer vitamins and minerals than Drink; it also had much less sugar. "Sometimes I wouldn't even put my phone in my bag, you know? If I was expecting a text, or if I hadn't hit my content goals." She began tearing the peeled-off label into strips. "You know the algorithms reward the people who post more often, right? It has to be multiple times a day, and it can't be predictable." The strips became smaller and smaller. "Which means you can't schedule your posts in advance, unless you're really careful about making everything look, like, *spontaneous*, and I'm not even sure that works anymore. I think they can tell if it's scheduled." One of the strips fluttered off the edge of the table. Bonnie did not pause to pick it up. "They want organic, real-time interaction, and it has to be all different kinds of content— like, you can't do *just photo* or *just text*, you have to do photo and video and text and replies and stories and shares and threads and everything else, if you want to even *rank*—and so I guess what I'm saying is that I always have my phone out, you know?"

"Right," Larkin said. She reached down and grabbed the scrap of bottled-water label, to save her coworkers from having to clean it up later. "You're saying it could have been anyone."

"I guess," Bonnie said. "But wouldn't it have had to be

someone who was in my class? Since, you know, that's when the music stopped?"

"I don't know," Larkin said. "It seems like it would have been really obvious if someone was poking around at your phone while class was going on."

"Yeah," Bonnie said, picking up the largest remaining piece of bottled-water label and tearing it in half. "I guess that was a bad idea."

"Not necessarily," Larkin said. "What if someone got into your accounts before class started?" She remembered how much time Bonnie usually spent greeting students; if someone had wanted to hack her unattended phone, they would have had plenty of opportunity. "It would be nice if we could get some security footage or something."

"Oh wow," Bonnie said, as if Larkin were in fact the best private detective ever. "That is a really good idea. How do we do it?"

"I was just going to ask you that question," Larkin said. "Do you know anything about how their security cameras work?" Everything she knew about security cameras came from police procedurals with craggy actors in reflective sunglasses. "Do they re-record over old footage? Or keep all the tapes lined up in a closet somewhere?"

"All I know is what was on the contract," Bonnie said. "By joining the Pratincola Fitness Complex, you are giving the organization the right to record your likeness at any time while on the premises and/or while participating in official Pratincola Fitness Complex activities, as well as nonexclusive access to use said likeness in future marketing materials." She smiled, asymmetrically, and finally sipped her water. "Or something like that. It's not like I have it memorized or anything. Basically they're saying they can put you on social whenever they want."

"Gotta get those likes," Larkin said. Then she stood up. "There's one more thing I gotta get—sorry—one more thing I *need to get* before I can start going after the security footage. Want to meet me at the fitness center at 4:30? Maybe we can get this done before they switch to after-hours staff."

Bonnie looked at The Coffee Shop's clock, which currently read *time for coffee* to *time for coffee*. The second hand moved two more times before she answered. "Um... sure?" Larkin refrained from asking Bonnie what time she thought it actually was, since she was pretty sure Bonnie hadn't consulted an analog clock since first grade. "I should go home first," Bonnie said, standing to match Larkin and picking up her coat and bag.

"Where do you live?" Larkin asked, suddenly wondering if this should have been her first question instead of her last one.

"The apartment complex on 28th," Bonnie said. "Near Howell."

Larkin knew the building, if only by reputation; if she weren't living with her mother, she'd probably be stuck there as well, stacked between adults who couldn't afford to live anywhere else and college students who didn't want to. "Did you go to school there?"

"Yeah," Bonnie said. "Me and my sister. We thought about going to different schools, but, I mean, you know."

Larkin didn't know. She wanted to, but she also wanted to get upstairs and get a very important question answered before it was time to go back to the fitness center and start asking for security footage. "Let's put a pin in this," she said, regretting the idiom the instant it popped out of her mouth. Nothing was more deflating than repro-ducing her mother's phrases, even though Dean Day would probably have been proud of the progenitation. "See you in two hours and fifteen minutes?"

Bonnie angled her face towards the clock for the second time. "Right," she finally said, putting her hands together. "Because it's a quarter past two."

———

Larkin took the elevator, this time—she wasn't about to run up five flights of stairs, even though she knew it would probably do her good, because what she needed to do was talk to Anni as quickly as possible and, like, maybe use her laptop.

And her printer.

And any envelopes and stamps she happened to have lying around, not that Anni ever left anything lying around. Anni hated lying, in all its forms, especially when it was supposed to be *laying*—but she no longer took direct objection to intransitive answers. As Larkin exited the elevator, she realized that Anni had become okay with equivocating, which was almost the same thing.

Then she heard noises coming from Anni's apartment. This, in itself, was not unusual; Anni was always talking to her plants or singing to herself or thumping away at her digital piano, and at first Larkin thought it was some combination of *thumping and talking,* or *thumping and singing,* or *thumping and singing a duet,* maybe—and then she heard a *creak* and an *oh* that cracked the code, revealing the verbs both in progress and in congress.

The pro: Anni, who never lied, was getting laid.

The con: Larkin was standing right outside the door.

This was extremely unusual, and Larkin's first instinct was to get herself out of the situation while she could still remain in good standing—but it was too late, there were already two pairs of feet approaching the lock, two eyes approaching the keyhole, a single voice, "it's Larkin," but by the time Anni opened the door it wasn't, anymore, because Larkin was following the safety instructions mounted on the wall next to the elevator and was running, for the second time that day, down five flights of stairs.

"We may have a problem," Larkin told Bonnie, when the two of them met up at the fitness center an hour later. Larkin had used her time to fail to answer the question she had been hoping to ask Anni, which was *can I ask a business to turn over its security footage even if I am not a licensed detective, and if not, can we file the business licensing paperwork right now?* If Larkin were still operating as an amateur detective, she could have tried finagling the footage out of whomever was behind the counter. By establishing her intent to go pro, she had inadvertently limited her prospects—at least until her business was officially established. Anni and Claire had explained, each in their own way, that she could get in *serious legal trouble* for practicing private investigation without a license.

"The state of Iowa allows licensed private investigators to report unlicensed private investigators," Anni had said. "It's unclear whether other people can report unlicensed private investigators as well, but we should assume that's the case." She sipped her tea. "Pun intended, as your boyfriend would say."

Larkin's mother's girlfriend had said much the same thing, although Claire had been holding a beer at the time. "You'll probably want to hold off on the sleuthing until you get the paperwork filed," Claire explained. "You may also want to get some firearms training." Larkin's mother, who was on her second glass of red wine, had insisted that Larkin would never-ever-ever need to carry, use, or even *understand* firearms. "My daughter will solve crimes using her *little gray cells.*" Claire had also suggested Larkin look into the Iowa Association of Private Investigators, which Josephine approved. "It'll be a good way to decide whether you want to be a detective."

"I do," Larkin had said. "I mean, that's the plan."

"But not if the plan includes *carrying a gun,* right?"

"A firearm is a tool," Claire had said. "Same as a desk or a phone."

"You can't hurt anyone with a phone!" Larkin's mother had argued—and then the three of them had spent the rest of the evening coming up with all the ways that one *could.* None of them even came close to suggesting that you could use a phone to erase a person's online identity, leaving them virtually murdered.

Pun intended, as Larkin's kinda-sorta-boyfriend might have said.

All of this meant that although Larkin knew exactly what she could do to get the footage Bonnie needed (the March 2022 Iowa Association of Private Investigators newsletter had an entire article on how to collect expirable evidence, such as security camera footage, without a search warrant or subpoena) she was pretty sure she couldn't take any of the recommended actions.

Not legally, anyway.

But maybe Bonnie could.

"Do you know who's in charge of the security cameras?" Larkin asked, wondering just how much she could get Bonnie to do before it became, like, entrapment or something. For her, of course. Bonnie would probably be fine.

"I could find out," Bonnie said. Larkin watched, from

what she hoped was a legally appropriate distance, as Bonnie approached one of the young people who took turns working—or, more likely, volunteering—at the fitness complex registration desk. Bonnie asked a few questions, and then the young person went off to find a slightly older person who knew the answers.

"They save security camera footage for two weeks," Bonnie told Larkin, once she had completed the aspect of the investigation she didn't know she had been tasked with.

"Great," Larkin said. This would give her plenty of time to file her licensing paperwork and draw up a preservation letter to prevent the footage from being erased.

"But there are no security cameras in my classroom," Bonnie said. "Only over the entrances and exits and, like, in the locker rooms."

"Okay," Larkin said. "That might make things a little more difficult, but—"

"But you knew that already," Bonnie said, as if she were the detective instead of Larkin. "That's why you said there might be a problem!"

"Right," Larkin said. Bonnie was not the brightest bulb in the Pratincola fitness center's fluorescent lighting system, but her memory appeared to be as strong as her quads. "I did say there might be a problem."

"Can you solve it by Friday?"

Larkin had forgotten about Bonnie's deadline. "That's, like, tomorrow." She took her phone out of her mother's coat pocket, to text Claire and invite her to come over for dinner. She didn't want to say *we probably won't get this done by Friday*, and she didn't want to say *I may have to ask my mother's girlfriend, who is a police officer, about the legal ramifications of continuing this investigation*, and then she didn't have to worry about what to say next because what she actually said was "I got a text from Anni."

"Who?"

"She's—"

"I know," Bonnie said, smiling again, "she's in my class. That was a joke. Anni is the one with the pixie cut and glasses. She helps new students, and she was kissing that guy after class on Monday."

"She was *what*?"

"It was intense," Bonnie said. "They looked like they were long-lost lovers or something."

That, at least, explained why Anni had failed to follow Ed and Larkin out to the parking lot on Monday. It might even explain the text Larkin had received: *do you want to meet him?*

Sure, Larkin texted back.

The next text both arrived from—and contained—an unknown number.

41.9738 N

She texted Anni.

Did you just text me?

The response arrived—but not from Anni.

91.6651 W

Larkin texted Anni again.

Someone just sent me two numbers was that you

The response came from the second number.

Red or white?

This time Larkin texted the new number directly.

Who are you?

Red or white?

Red.

That makes it your move. You have your coordinates. Pick a car, any car.

"What's going on?" Bonnie asked.

Larkin was about to respond—and then she finally got a response from Anni.

if you are going to be a licensed private detective you should be able to solve this

see you soon

CHAPTER 9

Larkin deduced, once she put the coordinates into her phone, that Anni and the person who had asked *Red or white?* were inviting her to dinner in Cedar Rapids. She suspected—correctly, as it turned out—that the person whom she did not know would have ginger hair, and he would have ordered a bottle of red wine for the table. She also suspected that this person didn't know that Anni didn't drink, but when she arrived at the restaurant she saw four wine glasses, three of which were already poured.

Three faces, two of which she already knew.

Two men standing up to greet her, one of which she was not expecting *at all.*

But of course Ed would be there. Of course Ed would lean forward to kiss Larkin's cheek and then reach behind her to pull out her chair—"did you know all of the chairs in this restaurant are hand-crafted," Anni said, since somebody had to say something—and then introduce her to Anni's new friend Elliott and pour her glass of wine.

Because this was, as it turned out, a double date.

If Larkin had been the licensed private detective that Anni and Ed and everyone else in her life still thought she might become, she might have been able to figure that one out. She might have gone home first, to change out of her barista clothing and into something a little more date-appropriate—but Anni was wearing the same basic sweater-and-leggings outfit she wore every day and Elliott was wearing some kind of collared shirt underneath a sweatshirt that read *Champaign Chess Club*. Ed, in gray cashmere and black jeans, was the only one who looked like he had put any effort into his appearance. Larkin didn't know if it was for her, for Anni and Elliott, or for all of the people who still saw Ed as CR's Newest Star. She sat down at their table and watched a Black couple one table over do a double-take; they immediately began whispering to each other, undoubtedly about *why that handsome Black man was on a double date with three average-looking white people*.

Elliott also saw the glance. "You're probably wondering how I know Anni," he said, effortlessly changing the subject. "We were friends—more than friends, really—about ten years ago."

"It was a cruise-ship romance," Anni said, taking the tiniest sip of her wine and setting it down again. "Statistically, they happen much more often than you think."

"Was it a singles cruise?" Ed asked.

"No," Anni said. "It's a nerd cruise."

"So you're a nerd," Ed said, smiling at Elliott.

Elliott grinned right back. "What gave it away—the bent spoon or the chess club shirt?"

"I think it was the fact that you texted me coordinates instead of an address," Larkin said. She noticed, for the first time, an angled spoon next to Elliott's place setting.

He must have been entertaining Ed and Anni before she arrived. "Or, like, *the name of the restaurant.*"

"Anni said you liked figuring things out," Elliott said. "Was she right?"

Larkin wasn't sure if she was supposed to reference what she had figured out earlier that afternoon—that Anni had been having sex with a geeky ginger who thought that bending spoons was a good way to pass the time. She waited to see whether either of them would bring it up, and then their conversation was brought to a close by a server with an open notebook.

"Looks like everyone's arrived," the server said. She asked the usual questions about appetizers and entrees, and then asked Elliott if he'd been to the restaurant before. "I swear I recognize you."

"It's my first time in Cedar Rapids," Elliott said, "but my date says we've picked the best place in town." Elliott smiled at Anni—Larkin watched his eyes crinkle, then soften—and turned back to the server. "Do you have a signature dish you'd like to recommend?"

"If you've never been here before, you should definitely get the Iowa pork chop," the server said, before launching into a spiel about specials. Elliott duly changed his order, and the server dutifully went away—but not without giving Anni's date a quick, backward glance.

Larkin's date, meanwhile, still meant to get the details of *how Anni and Elliott met.* "One of you needs to explain this to me," Ed said. "What's a nerd cruise?"

"It's just like an ordinary cruise," Anni said. "Staterooms, ports of call, multi-course dinners that require formalwear, that kind of thing. Except it's themed for nerds."

"All right," Ed said, "but there are many different kinds of nerds."

"And there are many different kinds of nerd cruises," Elliott said, holding out the wine bottle and offering Ed the last bit of red. "This one is themed around music, math, and magic."

"So no superheroes," Ed said. "And no Dungeons and Dragons."

"There's always Dungeons and Dragons," Anni said. "But the last time I went there was a four-hour seminar on the mathematics of D&D, and what Dungeon Masters needed to do to create games that had actual stakes." She took another, slightly larger, sip of wine. "In most cases Dungeons and Dragons is impossible to lose. There are so many safeguards built into the game mechanics that it's very difficult for anything negative, let alone *permanently negative*, to happen to your character. This is, of course, to attract more casual players. The people who are in it for, you know, the opportunity to eat chips all afternoon."

"And friendship!" Elliott said. "One must never forget about the power of friendship."

"One mustn't," Anni said, "but true friendship is only achieved through *achievement*. If you're playing a game in which you'll always defeat the dragon simply because the rule book has already decided that your characters will always be stronger than the dragon, unless you critical fail 20 times in a row, which, I can't remember the precise odds, or even the imprecise ones—"

"It's 1 to the 20th twenty times," Elliott said.

"I know *that*," Anni said. "I just can't come up with a good way to Fermi-estimate the exact number."

"Consider it equivalent to zero," Elliott said.

"Anyway," Anni said again, before—and after—taking another drink. "Anyway, the point is that once you build a character it is *equivalent to zero* that anything bad will happen to it, even if your character has incredibly bad stats, unless the DM is committed to a stakes-based game."

"Often involving actual stakes!" Elliott said. "The spiky kind."

"So did you meet playing Dungeons and Dragons?" Ed was very interested in pulling the conversation back towards general interest.

"No," Anni said. "I played once, but it took up so much time that I had to deliberately sacrifice my own character just to get out of it. Because there's no way for the game to end, and it's so boring if everything you do just results in you killing another dragon, and I had, like —" She was very nearly to the bottom of her glass. "My sister had just had twins, and here I was going over to that grody old apartment building, the one next to Howell, every weekend, to do this thing where we just sat around a circle and said, you know, *I cast a spell*."

"Tell them what you did," Elliott said. "It's a great story."

"Well," Anni said, "I told the DM first. I didn't want him to ruin anything by, like, dropping a healing potion at the last minute. Then, the next time we were at an inn, I picked a fight with one of the barkeeps. My character was Chaotic Good, so it was okay." She tried to take another drink and realized her wineglass was empty. "And then, we had this fight, the whole bar got involved, and because these were all NPCs instead of rulebook dragons the DM could choose the stats, and he finally made it difficult enough that we wouldn't automatically win, and it was the first time the game was fun, that moment when everyone else in the room realized that they wouldn't automatically win, and then I heroically exploded myself to save the rest of the party."

She picked up her wineglass, examined it carefully, and

put it down again. "And then I failed three saving throws. On purpose."

"Wait," Larkin said. "You cheated?" Anni didn't cheat —but she didn't drink, either, and she didn't date, and she didn't drive, and she didn't have sex, and yet Larkin was pretty sure that Anni had done all of the above, in reverse order, in the past twenty-four hours.

"Do you know how hard it is to permanently delete a Dungeons and Dragons character?" Anni said. "It's way harder than permanently deleting someone's online presence."

This brought the conversation around to Larkin, Bonnie, the murder, the time limit—"she wants it solved by tomorrow afternoon"—and the limits of what Larkin could do without a private investigator license.

"Does she need you to figure out who did it," Elliott asked, "or does she just need online access to her instructor dashboard?"

"Well," Larkin said, "that would be a start."

"Then I'll get started on it," Elliott said. "If you don't mind adding a rogue to your party."

Anni leaned her head onto Elliott's shoulder. "Ell, love, you're a sorcerer."

"No, my dearest," Elliott said, setting Anni upright and squeezing her hand. "Never again."

Larkin heard Ed's whisper, in her ear—"Are you completely confused? Or is it just me?"—but before she could answer, the food arrived.

———

By the time the meal was over, Ed had satisfied his curiosity about how Elliott and Anni met—they were both on the nerd cruise, nearly a decade ago; after that Elliott had taken on a series of professional obligations, and after that Anni's mom had gotten sick, and life had continued to get in the way until they contrived a way to get together again. Elliott was also satisfied, having successfully developed a plan to get Bonnie into her fitness dashboard by her Friday afternoon class—assuming that Larkin could pass a message to Bonnie through the Pratincola Fitness Complex cubby network. Anni had been satisfied ever since her single glass of wine. Larkin was the only one who remained temporarily unresolved.

Was Anni becoming one of those girls who completely changed herself for a guy? Larkin asked herself, as she made the ten-mile drive back to Pratincola. *And, like, for this guy?* Larkin barely knew Elliott, although she still felt like she had seen him somewhere before—but right now he was a solid B, solid and boring, nothing to *completely change yourself* about. If Elliott were able to help Bonnie run her fitness class as scheduled, she'd consider upgrading her estimation.

And what if Anni was right—which she usually was—and whatever she was doing was in fact the path to a solid relationship? Did that mean Larkin needed to think about changing herself for Ed? Larkin already drank, of course. She said actual swear words, instead of the garden-variety expletives ("oh, *shishito peppers*") that Anni had used ever since the birth of her nephews. She could even rat her hair —sometimes it ratted itself—and she had a pair of leather pants somewhere in her mother's guest bedroom, if they wanted to complete the *Grease* reference. Larkin couldn't think of anything she could add to make herself more attractive to Ed, in part because she wasn't at all sure why he found her attractive in the first place.

But he had agreed to the date, and he had worn the sweater she had given him for Christmas.

Even though he hadn't invited her to his family's Christmas party.

Larkin was this close, as she pulled into her mother's driveway, to asking her mother about it. Josephine and Claire were still together, after all, even though neither of them had really changed much about who they were. One of them read Neil Postman and the other read Neil Gaiman, one of them drank coffee and the other drank coffee-flavored beer, one of them didn't own a television and the other had seen every single season of *America's Got Talent*, and they were still able to make it work. Why couldn't Larkin?

But—just as Larkin was thinking of the best way to start the conversation—she saw something else she needed to ask her mother about.

Something more important.

Something that could change everything.

The sign that Josephine had put in the yard, two years ago—the one that listed all of the values the people in this house believed, even though Josephine had argued that one couldn't simply *believe* in a value, one had to *act on it*— had been defaced.

Or, more accurately, refaced.

The piece of paper taped to the front half of the sign read *ACAB*.

The piece of paper taped to the back half—the one facing the front window—read *RESIGN.*

CHAPTER 10

She wanted to rip the paper from its posting; instead, Larkin pulled the posts out of the ground and carried the entire sign—the *resign* side pressed to her chest—into her mother's house.

Josephine was already there, of course. So was Claire, pacing circles around the kitchen table. She paused when she saw Larkin, placing one hand on Josephine's shoulder and another on the scritchy spot between Pal's ears.

"Good girl," Claire said. It could have been meant for Pal. It could have been meant for Larkin, who followed her instincts and deposited the sign in the closet of her mother's guest bedroom before returning to the kitchen, where Josephine—following Larkin's initiative—was standing up and throwing away a pile of used tissues.

"Good girl," Claire said again. Pal padded to her spot by the doorway. Larkin took her seat at the table. Josephine washed her hands and then tried to figure out what to do with them; Larkin watched her mother cross her arms, uncross them, and place her hands hesitantly on her hips.

"What are we going to do?" Josephine asked. One hand went to her hair, pushing a stray piece behind her ear. The other wiped carefully at her left eye. She sniffed. Claire held out the tissue box, but Josephine shook her head. "We're going to think," she said, decisively—although her decision looked less impressive after she looked to Claire and Larkin for approval. "And then we're going to do something."

"You could just let this blow over," Larkin said. She had seen the way these conflicts played out online: a pile-on, an apology, an abdication of responsibility. Not the kind of situation she wanted her mother to participate in, if non-participation were still a possibility.

"They've already escalated," her mother said. "This person has *made a demand*."

"Which means you wait," Claire said. "The worst thing you could do right now is give this person attention. That gives them the power, and that's how you get real escalation. Withholding attention forces their hand. They're either going to try again, with the hope of getting some kind of response, or they're going to back off and find something else to do."

"So you're saying I do nothing."

"Yes," Claire said. "My professional recommendation is that you do nothing."

"Should I put the sign back in the yard?" Larkin asked.

"No," Claire said, "that's fine. If another sign shows up, at the house or at Howell, one of you can take it down. But don't make a big deal out of it. Don't swear, or cry, or tear it up. Treat it like a piece of everyday garbage—like somebody's newspaper that accidentally ended up in your yard—and calmly remove it from the premises."

Josephine nodded, accepting Claire's suggestion to remain calm—or to resemble a calm person, at a glance.

She scooped up her wayward, graying hair, restoring it in a loop of rubber band before she realized Claire was really suggesting. "You think they're watching us." Any semblance of calm vanished. "Watching *me*, to see how I react."

"They could be."

"And you still think I should do nothing?"

Claire shook her head. "I've seen these kinds of situations before. Usually an ex-lover. Occasionally it's someone who's trying to get a job. They send messages or they make phone calls or they follow you around, maybe for a few weeks, maybe for a few months, and as long as you don't respond they eventually stop."

"What if I do respond?"

"Then they've just learned that it takes two hand-written signs to get you to respond." Claire squeezed Josephine's shoulder. "I've seen way worse. I had to tell this woman, once, *look, if you do anything right now he'll know that it takes fifty phone calls to get you to respond.* She'd been getting these calls for nearly a year. I got her not to give in."

"Then what happened?"

"The calls stopped," Claire said. "She got two more and that was it. He moved on."

Larkin watched her mother calm down again. Claire was very good at what she did. Nobody who knew Officer Novak would ever think she was a bastard—and then Larkin watched her mother, who was watching her, as they both recognized what neither of them had remembered.

"We already responded," Josephine said, twisting away from Claire and calm. "You said it was okay!"

"When did I say—"

"When I said I could figure out who had made those

social media posts," Larkin said. "The ones about the two of you at Pancake Breakfast." She turned to her mother, who was digging another tissue out of the box. "Mom, it's okay, Ghoti was actually kind of cool, and I thought we had a really good conversation."

"And maybe all we did is convince this student that it only takes one sign to get a response!"

"Maybe," Larkin said. She opened her phone and began checking Ghoti's feeds. There hadn't been a single negative post about Howell or any of its faculty or administrators since Larkin had caught Ghoti in the campus bookstore. This, in and of itself, should have been proof that her investigation was successful. That Claire wasn't the only person who was good at what she did. That Ghoti —whose social media feeds suggested they were in the middle of some kind of '80s movie marathon—was *probably not the person who had posted the second sign.*

Larkin gave her mother their sign—a quick nose twitch —followed by a display of Ghoti's most recent online activity. "I may have chased down the wrong suspect," she said, handing the phone over to Josephine to scroll.

"Who has time to watch three movies on a Thursday night?" Josephine asked, perusing Ghoti's musings. "And why is anyone still wasting their time on *Dead Poets Society*?"

"Oh captain, my captain!" Larkin and Claire said at the same time.

"That movie didn't do a thing for poetry," Josephine said. "Neither of you know the next line, right?"

"Nope," Claire said.

"And neither of you know the poet."

"Nope," Larkin said.

"I rest my case," Josephine said, twitching her nose back at Larkin.

"Well, I'm not going to rest mine," Larkin said. "I'm going to talk to Ghoti again. I mean, if you don't mind." That was directed mostly towards Claire, although it was Josephine who answered first. "I don't mind. Look!" She turned the phone around so Larkin and Claire could see. "They actually understand that Mr. Keating is misinterpreting Robert Frost! You should talk to them. I should talk to them! Maybe I can get Janessa to set up a meeting."

"Which one is Janessa?" Claire asked.

"She's my assistant," Josephine said. "She's amazing. We've been doing this student assistant program for a while, application-only, class credit. Of course it's really an opportunity for Howell to save money on salary costs, but we frame it as an opportunity for the student, the chance to become a student-leader, and it is! It really is." Larkin watched her mother try to convince them all that class credit for a student was better than a full-time job for an adult. Nobody believed it—least of all Josephine. "Janessa's the first one who's been able to help me more than I've had to help her," her mother finished, handing the phone back to Larkin.

"Should I tell Ghoti to talk to Janessa, then?"

"If you want," Josephine said. "I mean, if Claire thinks it's okay."

"If there's one thing I know about sleuths," Claire said, "it's that they never pick the right person the first time. If you want to go tell this student you made a mistake, fine—but maybe don't talk to anyone else at Howell about this, okay?"

"So, like, not Ed."

"Definitely not Ed," Claire said. "Sorry."

That got Larkin off the hook, at least temporarily, from having to ask Ed whether he thought all cops were bastards. She'd go to the campus bookstore tomorrow and apologize for putting Ghoti on the hook—and fish, just a little, for information.

"How is Ed?" Larkin's mother asked. "He told me the two of you had a date tonight."

"That's why she didn't call," Claire said. "About the sign."

"I wanted to," Josephine said. "But Claire said it wouldn't make a difference, and we should let you enjoy the evening."

"Oh," Larkin said. Sometimes she forgot how thoughtful her mother could be, especially now that Claire was around to help her think about things besides academia. "Thank you." In return, Larkin opened the photo app on her phone and showed them the picture their server had taken—after Anni, giddy on a glass of red wine, had asked them to *commemorate the moment*. It had taken Anni three tries to get the word *commemorate* out in one piece; the server should have taken at least as many attempts with Larkin's app, or maybe Larkin should have suggested they take a group selfie. That way she could have gotten a shot that showed the night they should have had—two delighted couples, out on a double date— instead of a picture that revealed two happy faces and two less-than-happy ones.

"Ed looks like he's having a really good time," Larkin's mother said, passing the phone to Claire. "He's been so stressed out lately. I'd say *take him out again*, but I'm not sure I'm allowed to say that. Not as his dean, for sure. Probably not even as your mother."

"I'll say it," Claire said. "Take him out again." Then she paused, and pried at the fourth face with her fingers until it expanded into recognition. "Wait—what were the three of you doing with Scarbo?"

"Who's Scarbo?" Josephine asked.

"Scarbo's a magician," Claire said. "Don't you remember? He was on TV—like, real TV, *network television*—for nearly a year."

"You're right," Larkin said. She had known as soon as Claire said the name. She wondered if Anni knew.

"And then there was this disaster," Claire continued. "Live. *On-air.* How do you not remember this?"

"I don't have a TV," Josephine said. "You know that."

"It doesn't matter," Claire said. "It was all we were talking about, the next day. In the office."

It was all Larkin and her friends had been able to talk about, too. She had been in her first year of grad school, in Los Angeles. Scarbo had announced, the previous week, that he was going to prove—well, Larkin had a hard time describing it then and would have an even harder time describing it now, it had something to do with the universe being either inconsistent or incomplete but not *both*, and as Claire pulled up the video on her tablet and set it on the table to watch it all came back, the young magician with red-gold hair, androgynous and ambidextrous, connecting and deflecting and explaining and maintaining this patter as the pattern of shadows behind him shifted.

Magic became *logic*.

Complete became *inconsistent* became *incomplete* became *consistent*.

"But this is just shadow-magic," Scarbo said, snapping his fingers. The room became dark; his face appearing only by the flame that he appeared to be holding between the thumb and third finger of his left hand. Larkin knew—or assumed, anyway—that there was a very tight spot involved. "Platonic," Scarbo said. "What we know derives entirely from what we can remember, and you've already forgotten whether *incomplete* came before *inconsistent* or whether it was the other way around."

He had performed this—live on television, and live onstage—before people began offloading the responsibility of remembering to a mnemonic system that made knowledge non-binary; before a person like Larkin's mother, who had protected and preserved her powers of retention, was able to say "Scroll back, I'm sure it was *inconsistent* and then *incomplete*," and a person like Claire, who had retained the power to protect and serve, could offer the proof.

"Nice job, prof," she said.

"Nice job, officer," Josephine said back.

"It is the act of forgetting," Scarbo continued, once he had been restored to his position, "the fact that our memories are consistent but incomplete—or is it the other way around—that allows people like me to create the kinds of logical inconsistencies that people like you call *magic*. All I am doing is using a girdle application—"

"Pause that," Josephine said. "They captioned it wrong! He means *Gödel*. The famous mathematician. The one who created the incompleteness theorem, or whatever it is. I can't remember it exactly."

"Keep watching," Claire said, tapping the button to start the video again. "It's just about to get good."

She meant that it was about to get bad.

Very, very bad.

"All I am doing is using a girdle application to demonstrate that—well, you've already forgotten, haven't you?"

He paused, just long enough to give the audience a chance to fail to answer.

"How tall I am."

At this point Scarbo holds the candle flame out, in his

left hand, as if to measure his own height; his face disappears, and only his fingers are visible.

"Whoops!" he says. "You can't see me."

He snaps again. Another flame appears, between the fingers of his right hand; his face is noticably higher than the previous measurement, and the distance between hand and head appears to be increasing.

"You might also try to remember how long my arms are." The hand holding the second flame stretches out. His face disappears and the distance between his right- and left-hand fingertips becomes anatomically impossible.

"And how many hands I have." A third set of fingers snaps into position; a third flame lights his face, which is now closer to the flies than the footlights.

"Am I inconsistent?" Another flame flies off to the side of the stage; another snap, and a fourth hand takes its place in front of his face. "Or are you incomplete?" The fourth hand is sent to the opposite side of the stage; the fifth hand puts Scarbo's face at the apex of the pentagram. "Is the universe what it appears to be, or is what you see nothing more than apparition?"

He pauses, one last time.

"I am a magician, which means I can make things disappear."

The four discorporate hands snap their fingers and vanish.

"It also means I can make myself disappear."

A fifth snap. The stage is dark again.

"And reappear."

Lights up. Scarbo is walking confidently towards the front of the stage. "And now," he says, "we are ready to have a conversation about magic, logic, illusion, and truth. From this point on, what you see *can* be believed."

If he hadn't said that, what happened next wouldn't

have been quite so unbelievable. First the scream, then the scrim—dropping, draping itself over one of the suspended stagehands, catching itself on another of the stagehands, and then catching on fire. The assistant stage manager runs onstage with the fire extinguisher, and although the stagehand is able to smother the fire before the stage manager gets the nozzle aimed, the protocol is followed to completion.

"And that was the end of his career," Claire said, pausing the video.

"Well," Josephine said. "I suppose I do have to believe what I just saw." That was the joke Larkin remembered everyone making—but she also remembered something else.

"There's more video, isn't there?" she asked.

"Just the apology," Claire said.

This, Larkin understood—in a way she hadn't, a decade ago, when she was laughing over his disaster with her grad school classmates—was the real reason why Scarbo's career as a magician had ended. "We should watch it," she said.

"I tire of television," her mother said. "It's so *dreadful*." She gave Claire a quick kiss. "I'm going to bed."

"I'll be in," Claire said, "in a minute." She stowed her tablet, carefully, in its sleeve. "Nice job helping me calm her down. You're a good kid."

"Thanks," Larkin said. She took out her phone. "You don't mind that I'm going to talk to Ghoti tomorrow, right? That won't compromise Mom's safety or anything?"

"I don't see any reason to be concerned about your mother's safety," Claire said. "Not yet."

"Great," Larkin said. "Now you're going to make me worry about the *yet* part."

"Sorry," Claire said, smiling. "Go distract yourself by

asking your friend if she knows she's dating a guy who used to have his own TV show."

Now Larkin smiled. "How did you know I was going to do that?"

"You're not the only sleuth in the house," Claire said, squeezing Larkin's shoulder. "And if he can get us dinner with anyone who was on *Firefly*, let me know." She bent to pet Pal, who padded with her out the door. "I have a soft spot for lost causes."

"Sure," Larkin said. She had already sent the text—*did you know you are dating Scarbo*—and Anni had already responded.

Obviously. I named him.

The next message Larkin sent consisted entirely of question marks.

The next message Anni sent was an email.

Subject line: *Since you (finally) asked.*

CHAPTER 11

Dear Larkin—

I am writing this on December 1.

Does that surprise you, on whatever day you might be reading it?

It shouldn't surprise you that I had this planned, of course. You can't spell planning without Anni, after all—or at least that's what my mother likes to say.

But it should surprise you to remember that in all this time you never asked.

You might not even remember what you were supposed to have asked. We were at the fundraising gala, for the symphony, right after you solved your first murder. The one where we all came in costume.

That morning, I got my first email from Elliott in ten years.

You asked me what had happened—because you could tell something had happened. You are much better than I am at uncovering emotion, and I am not very good at hiding it.

I said I'd tell you if you promised not to tell anyone that I was wearing my skeleton pajamas as a Halloween costume.

You agreed—but the next day, when you and I met up for our usual cups of whatsit, all you wanted to talk about was you.

And Ed.

And you-and-Ed.

And so the evening passed without your ever asking, and I didn't realize it until after you'd gone.

That was all fine, of course. I was only disappointed after the fact, and not for very long, and I can't say we didn't have a good time together because if I hadn't had a good time, you would have noticed it.

And then of course I still thought you might ask the next time we met up.

This is where you and I are different. This is where everyone-and-Anni are different, really. I would have written it down in my notebook, and I would have carried it over from page to page until it got done, and then I would have crossed it off.

I don't know what you would have done.

I only know what you actually did—which is to say that we continued to meet in my apartment building, as we always had, and we continued to discuss your life, as we always had.

And now you know what I did.

I decided not to say a word about Elliott until you asked me about him.

And then—and this was Elliott's idea—I decided not to tell you that Elliott had once been Scarbo until you figured it out on your own.

Now I will tell you everything.

Elliott Fox and I met on the nerd cruise. It was the first of these cruises, not only for the two of us but also for the organization running the event. There weren't enough attendees to book the entire ship; that year, only 150 people registered. This turned out to be fortuitous, because we were able to make our own Dunbar-friendly group among the vacationers and retirees.

It was exceptionally fortuitous for Elliott—but that's telling the end of the story before the beginning. The middle of the story, really, since we are currently revisiting and revising what we had previously assumed was the conclusion.

We met during the lifeboat drill. He and I were sharing the same lifeboat, or at least we would have been if the lifeboats had ever been deployed. At any rate we were obliged to stand next to each other during the hour-long muster—and somehow we mustered up the courage to start talking to each other, and by the end of the exercise we were familiar not only with our lifesaving craft, but also our shared philosophies on life and craft.

Sorry—I'm getting writerly.

(Elliott likes it when I get writerly.)

At that time I was a freelance SEO copywriter who wanted to be a pianist and Elliott was a freelance software developer who wanted to be a magician. I fell in love with him the morning he picked the lock on the ship's lounge so I could practice—and no, it wasn't because he was able to do that little bit of entry-level magic, it was that he understood that I needed to practice, and I needed to practice in the early morning for it to do the most good, and I needed to go to bed early the night before so I could be ready for the morning session.

The cruise staff discovered us right away, of course. They let me continue playing. They told me that the next morning, the room would be open and ready for me. They told Elliott never to pick any locks onboard ship again.

This meant that he needed to change his magic show.

That first year, the cruise was so new that they didn't have enough programming, so they invited all of us attendees to sign up for twenty-minute performance slots. Elliott and I had both signed up, months in advance, and on that last day before the performance—the first full day we spent together, without need or care of anyone else—we went over his show and restructured it, substituting card tricks for lockpicks and writing new patter to cover his sleight of hand.

Then we spent our first full night together.

That was when I named him. He asked me if I would mind if he sat up and practiced while I slept, and I asked him if he would mind if I got up early to play the piano while he slept, and since neither of us minded—and since it was so comfortable, already, for both of us to ask for what we wanted—we proceeded with our plan. I woke up in the middle of the night to use the tiny state-room toilet, and there he was, a tiny booklight illuminating his fingers, and he asked me if he had woken me up and I said no, I always woke up ninety minutes after I fell asleep, he shouldn't worry, when I went back to bed I would sleep for a good four-hour chunk, and when I came out of the bathroom he kissed me, and I said—without thinking—"you should call yourself Scarbo."

He did not get the reference until I explained it the next morning. You will not until you look it up, and I suggest listening to the Martha Argerich recording. I do not suggest looking up the recording that the cruise ship took of my perfor-mance, first because the data is submerged under a decade's worth of uploads and second because both the video and my rendition of Gaspard de la Nuit *are fairly blurry.*

I am embarrassed, now, to have attempted it. Elliott says I shouldn't be. "You didn't unravel," he wrote, when he and I started writing again, and because of that I loved him the way I had ten years ago, when we were both young enough to think we could become exactly what we wanted.

You can watch Elliott's video, if you find it. It's quite good. At the time I thought he had something that I did not, which was true, but my error was calling that something "talent" instead of the more appropriate "years of work."

That was the first error I made, on that cruise.

The second error was not accompanying Elliott to the ship's bar afterwards. I went to bed, and Elliott went to the bar, and the next morning he told me that he had been approached by one of the Featured Guests—a magician who was also a neuroscientist, believe it or not—and the Guest had asked Elliott if he wanted to put together an opening act for his performance later that week.

I woke up that night to use the toilet and Elliott was there, shuffling and counting and planning the rest of the week. He kissed me and I went back to sleep. The next morning, after I had practiced—because of course you practice, even the morning after your performance, even on a cruise—he told me what had happened.

I was thrilled, of course. Even more so at the end of the week, when I saw him perform. By disembarkation day he had made plans to tour with the magician neuroscientist, just two weeks, he had enough vacation time saved to make it work, and I could come visit him when the tour hit Chicago.

Nothing is ever just two weeks.

I did visit him, in Chicago. We had a drink—because it was before my former teetotalism—and went to bed and he told me he was going to quit his job and pursue magic full-time, he had enough money saved to make it work, and he asked me whether I wanted to be a part of any of it.

He says this was his error—asking if I wanted to be a part instead of a partner.

My error—the third, if you're keeping track—was saying no.

Not because it was an incorrect choice, but because I chose incorrectly.

I held my liquor and looked at him and saw, instantly, what would happen—the tour, the television show, the opportunity to perform in front of some of the most famous magicians in the business. I didn't look like any of the women who hung around the kinds of magicians he was about to become. I didn't act like any of them, either. I would be a liability rather than an asset, and liable to get my heart broken.

So I broke it myself, at the bar, and the next time he wrote me, I didn't respond.

I should have.

I almost wish I had—but then I wonder whether I would have been there for my sister, when she needed me, or for my mother, when she needed all of us.

Then I wonder whether Elliott and I would have been there together, and how it might have gone if we had.

It all went very well, without him. Both my sister and my mother—especially my mother—would say as much. But as I watched my mother become less well, I did what I believed at the time to be the only rational thing: to read every peer-reviewed article on cancer and to strategically remove all potential carcinogens—alcohol, sugar, all of the best-tasting meats—while simultaneously keeping weight, heartrate, and sleep state within measure. I tried one of those three-day cancer-fighting fasts and nearly passed out.

If Elliott had been there, I might not have lost track of my life.

If I had been there, Elliott might not have lost track of his magic.

The disaster—I am assuming that you have seen the disaster —derived in part from network pressure and in part from Elliott not having the strength to say that his strength was in close-up magic, in connection, in illusion made real through physics and practicality. He never wanted pyrotechnics, only technique. He wanted to show people what could be done with just two hands.

Now we want to see what might happen if our hands work together.

You might ask how we got back in touch, if you were the kind of person who asked people about things that weren't directly related to murder investigations.

(I will ask Elliott, tomorrow, whether that is too harsh; if so, I will delete it.)

I had kept up with his life, off and on, the two states of a programmer's existence, always knowing he was one state away.

He had not kept up with me, but that was because he didn't know that I had also changed my name for professional reasons. Elliott kept looking for "Annie Morgan," and by the time he realized that I had deleted the e to improve retrieval—in search, in email, in memory—it was October.

And now it is whenever it is when you finally asked.

At this point you might think I am angry with you, for failing at some aspect of friendship. I am not. If friendship were a ledger, no one would ever be able to balance it. All I mean to say is that I see you failing to see people—me, Ed, your mother—and I suspect it is because you can't see yourself right now. Are you a detective or a barista? Was I a pianist or a copywriter? Both of these are the wrong questions, of course—but they prevent us from asking the more important ones.

Let me end this as I should have began it—

If I had accepted Elliott's invitation to join him at the cruise ship bar, all those years ago, I would have met the magician neuroscientist's wife. (This, by the way, would make an excellent book title.) I would have seen, for myself, that she was a perfectly lovely person—but no more beautiful than anyone else, and no more part of his act than any other partner. She taught high school. She wore glasses. She made quilts based on Penrose tilings.

Ask me how my life could have gone if I had known that.

Anni

CHAPTER 12

Larkin didn't know how to respond to Anni's email, so she didn't.

She didn't sleep much, either.

She did get up, with her alarm, in time to make her early-morning shift at The Coffee Shop.

As Larkin made her first pot of coffee—the one for the staff, to give them the energy to pull espressos and push pastries—she asked herself whether she should start asking people more questions.

"How was your evening?" she asked her boss.

That probably wasn't the kind of question Anni had in mind, but Larkin knew very little about her boss—which was probably the problem. How much were you supposed to know? Were you really supposed to ask your supervisor about their hopes and dreams? Her boss's evening had been "great!" and her boss would have said "great!" even if it hadn't been. That was all that needed to pass between them before they started passing cups to customers.

Larkin hadn't gotten any further on the question of *how to ask people more questions* by the time Elliott arrived. He ordered one cup of Earl Grey—he did not add the word "hot" at the end, which Larkin appreciated—and one cup of a Valentine's Day-themed hibiscus blend called Love Potion.

"I can't believe it's already February," Larkin said. It was the third time she'd said it this morning. This time she followed up with "Can you?"

This was also not the kind of question Anni wanted her to ask. Elliott did not respond, which made Larkin wonder how much he knew about the previous eight hours. He had to know enough to know that Larkin would feel terrible about asking what she knew she had to ask next— but it was Friday morning, and Bonnie's next fitness class was eight hours away.

"Remember how you said you could help Bonnie get into her dashboard?"

"Yes." Elliott seemed like the kind of person who would remember that.

"Would you be able to meet us at the fitness center at 3 p.m.?"

"Yes," Elliott said again. "See you then." He took a to-go cup in each hand. "Anni says hello."

"Say hello back," Larkin said. When Elliott was halfway to the door she called out "Tell her I'm thinking about what she wrote," in a voice loud enough to draw eyes from laptops and a frown from her boss. "Please," she added, since she had already projected herself into earshot. "And please tell her *thank you.*"

Elliott nodded. He knew everything, after all. She had suspected as much—and now she had to think about what she would say to her former suspect, assuming she could get to the campus bookstore as soon as her shift ended. Sometimes her boss asked people to stay late, and Larkin needed the job too much to say no—plus, she couldn't afford to turn down the extra hours. Anni had said that Larkin shouldn't think of her life as *director-or-barista*, after all.

No, wait.

Detective-or-barista.

Director was what she had wanted to be before all of this began.

Detective was what she was failing at being now.

Barista was what she had to be for the next three hours, even though all she really wanted to be was *asleep*.

———

Larkin was so tired that, three minutes after walking into the Howell College bookstore, she walked right up to a woman who reminded her of Bonnie Cooper and said "Did you get my message? I've got a friend who's going to meet us at the fitness center this afternoon."

"I'm sorry?" the woman said. She wore a Howell-branded sweatshirt and a lanyard embroidered with the word *staff*. "Can I help you?"

"No," Larkin said. "I guess I thought I could help you." It was a ridiculous thing to say, but it was also a ridiculous mistake to make—the woman had Bonnie's height and Bonnie's hair, but her face was sharper, with narrower eyes. She narrowed her eyes even further when Larkin asked "Is Ghoti on shift today?"

"They're on break," the woman said, and Larkin couldn't tell if this bookstore staff member was against breaks, or against Ghoti, or against whatever circumstances had put her in this position. She was not young enough to be a typical college student—"actually, ten percent of our student body are what we call *nontraditional students*,"

Larkin heard her mother say, the reminder winding its way through her sleep-deprived mind—and not old enough to have had a fulfilling career before spending her afternoons refilling pronoun button bins. Larkin wondered who this person had wanted to be, before she became who she was. She almost asked—Anni would have wanted her to ask, right?—and then the woman gestured towards a table in the corner of the bookstore.

Larkin was familiar with nontraditional breakrooms. She'd worked in enough theaters to know exactly what you had to do—and what you *didn't* have to do—to meet Equity standards. When Larkin's coffee shop shifts lasted longer than four hours, she took her state-mandated minutes in the corner of the kitchen or, if she felt like she could afford to treat herself, the other side of the counter. The location, or lack thereof, no longer mattered. In every real sense of the word, Larkin and every other employee she knew spent their breaks on their phones.

That was how Larkin found Ghoti—head down, fingers swiping.

"Hey," Larkin said. "I came to say—"

What had she come to say, anyway?

"I'm sorry, I think."

She hadn't meant that last part.

"You think?" Ghoti twisted towards Larkin. The smile was genuine, although Larkin couldn't tell if Ghoti was happy to see her or simply happy to have landed another zinger.

"Well, I'm not doing a very good job of it today," Larkin said. "But I think I did an even worse job the last time I was here."

"Why?" Ghoti pushed their hair out of their eyes just long enough to scrutinize Larkin. "I left your mom alone," they continued, the locks falling back into place. "Isn't that what you wanted?"

"I mean, sure," Larkin said. "That was a good thing for you to do. I appreciate it." Her thoughts were having the hardest time shaping themselves into sentences. "But I accused you of something you didn't do."

"No, you didn't."

"Yeah, I did," Larkin said. "Those signs."

Now it was Claire's voice, in her memory: "Don't let anyone know you're upset about the signs." That's what she'd said, right? That was how they were all supposed to protect Larkin's mother?

"I'm not upset about the signs," Larkin said. "My mom isn't either."

"Okay," Ghoti said, turning away from Larkin and back to their phone. "So you're not here to howl at me."

"No," Larkin began, "I—"

"That was a pun," Ghoti said. "A real one."

"Oh," Larkin said. *Howl at me.* "I guess it was."

"A lot of people say things are puns when they're really just jokes." Ghoti checked the time on their phone, and then put it into their pocket. "Not Dr. Jackson, though. Is that why you like him?"

"Um, no," Larkin said. *Why did she like Ed?* "I like him because he's smart."

"You like him because he's hot," Ghoti said. "And because he pays attention to you. Is that why your mom likes that cop?"

"I don't know," Larkin said. She was still trying to figure out why she liked Ed—and why Ghoti's question made her feel so sad. "I think Mom likes Claire because they take care of each other." That was right, Larkin knew, but it wasn't all of it. "And because they have the same idea about what people could become, if they wanted to."

That was closer. "What a good person could be." She watched Ghoti watching her, more interested in this answer than anything Larkin had said thus far. "They're both trying to be the same kind of good person."

"Okay," Ghoti said again. "I have to go back to work." They held out a hand, nail-bitten and ink-stained, to Larkin. "You can tell your mom that I'm sorry too."

"You can tell her yourself," Larkin said. "She wants to meet you. She says you should contact Janessa in her office to set up a time. Do you know Janessa?"

Ghoti raised their one visible eyebrow. "Everyone knows Janessa," they said. "That's, like, her whole deal."

"Well," Larkin said, "I'll leave you to deal with her." She waited to see if Ghoti got it.

"That's not really a pun," Ghoti said. "It's just a homonym." They pulled their *student-leader* lanyard out of their pocket and draped it over their neck. "But I'll tell your boyfriend that you're trying to be the same kind of person as him, if you want."

"I think we're good," Larkin said—hoping Ghoti wouldn't catch her in the lie.

———

Larkin caught up with Elliott and Bonnie a few minutes after three. They were in the lobby of the Pratincola Fitness Complex, Elliot's laptop spread over both their laps. His phone, on his free knee, was set to speaker.

"Yeah, it looks like her password was changed on Wednesday, February 1," the person on the other end of the phone said.

"Can we get a timestamp on that?" Elliott asked.

"Sure. The request went through at 5:03 p.m. Eastern."

"Location?"

"Pratincola, Iowa."

"Device?"

"Couldn't tell you. It came through the app, though."

"Not a web browser."

"Nope."

"Were there multiple instances running?"

"Of the app? Couldn't tell you."

"Tell me this, then," Elliott said, glancing up just long enough to nod his head at Larkin, "what do we need to do to get her back on?"

"Well, we'd need some way of proving it was her, you know?"

"Right," Elliott said. "And TFA's out because she's been locked out of text and email." He turned to Bonnie. "Does your phone still receive calls?"

"I don't know," Bonnie said. "I never thought of that."

"Right," Elliott said again. He tilted his voice towards his left knee. "Can you do a two-factor authentication through call?"

"Damn it, we used to," the voice said. "But we killed that option, like, five years ago."

"All right," Elliott said. He thought about this—they all watched him think, his fingers bouncing against his right knee, his chin rocking up and down—and then he spoke.

"Give me the options you didn't kill."

"What do you mean?"

"I know there's some way of getting in that's still built into the system," Elliott said. "Social media predates TFA and integrated user accounts. It predates smartphones, even. There's no way you killed everything you used before you switched to the systems you're using now, so you should have at least one legacy authentication protocol that doesn't require a phone or email and is still functional."

Then they all watched Elliott watch the phone. The other set of fingers tapped, then stopped.

"Jeez, Ell," the voice said, "you owe me."

"I'll give you five stars," Elliott said. "Your customer service is exceeding expectations."

"Ask her when she opened the account."

Elliott turned to Bonnie. "When did you open this account?"

"When I turned thirteen," Bonnie said. "But we had smartphones then. I got one for my birthday."

"Did you get a code?" the voice asked.

"For my birthday?"

"No," the voice asked. "When you opened the account. A six-digit backup verification code."

"Yes," Bonnie said. "We were supposed to write it down and put it in a safe place where nobody could ever find it."

"Right," the voice said. "Because that was how we still did security ten years ago."

"I kept it safe," Bonnie said.

"Right," the voice said again. "On a sticky note in your desk drawer, just like everybody else."

"No," Bonnie said. "In my head."

"You memorized it?" Elliott asked.

Bonnie smiled, putting her hand up to cover the side of her face that no longer matched the other. "It was easy. Zero-eight-three-two-three-five."

From there, it *was* easy—Elliott shifted his laptop onto Bonnie's lap, she used his browser to attempt to log into her old social media account, and when the login failed the voice on the other end of the phone helped Bonnie navigate to the part of the website where she could input her backup verification code.

"All it is," Bonnie said, "is, like, a zero becomes an

eight when you squish it, and then a three when you cut it in half, and then two plus three is five."

"Great," the voice said. "Are you in?"

"Not yet," Bonnie said. "It wants me to make a new password first."

"Don't make it any password you've ever used before," Elliott said. "You probably shouldn't even use dictionary words."

"Thanks, I know," Bonnie said, entering what Larkin hoped was a case-sensitive string of numbers, letters, and special characters. "Do you need to write it down?" she asked. "No," Bonnie said, filling out the confirmation field. "Thank you, I've got this, and—I'm in!"

"Wow," Larkin said. "That's impressive." She turned to Elliott. "I owe you at least a bottle of wine, or something."

"It's no big deal," Elliott said. "Bonnie needed access to one of her social media accounts before she could log into her fitness instructor dashboard—which isn't how I would have built it, but nobody asked me."

"We love it," the voice on the other end of the phone said. "You won't believe how many new users we got once all those smaller apps figured out they could use us to solve the login problem."

"And the profile problem."

"We solve a lot of problems," the voice said. "At least as many as we cause."

"I'm in my dashboard," Bonnie said. "I can run today's class!"

"Good," Elliott said. "You can use this laptop until we figure out how to get your OS accounts reactivated. System accounts are a little more complicated than social media, but I'll start thinking about how to get you in touch with someone who can help."

He picked up his phone. "Thanks again," he said.

"No problem," the voice replied. "Don't forget about the five-star rating."

"Wait," Larkin said. She couldn't believe she hadn't thought of this earlier. She could barely believe she'd thought of it at all. "The first time the password was changed—did the two-factor authentication go through text or email?"

"Who's that?" the voice asked.

"A friend," Elliott said. He nodded to Larkin. "That's a very good question. I should have thought to ask it."

"I can check that for you," the voice said.

They waited.

"It was text."

"So it would have had to have been done *on her phone,*" Larkin said.

"I couldn't say that for sure," the voice said, "but probably."

"Then I really, really need to apply for my business license," Larkin said, "because we're going to need access to those security cameras."

"You shouldn't apply for a business license just to get access to a security camera." It was Anni, dressed for Bonnie's workout because she had guessed—correctly—that Elliott would work everything out. Larkin was still wearing her barista clothing. She hadn't even thought about preparing herself for forty-five minutes of guided fitness.

She also hadn't thought about preparing herself for Ed —but there he was, gym bag over one shoulder, shaking hands with Elliott, saying hello to Bonnie and Anni. Larkin wanted to call out all of the questions she had inchoately collated: *Are you all right? My mom said you were stressed out? Do you want to talk about it? Does this have anything to do with me? Is there any way I can help? Why do you like me?*

Why do you think I like you? If someone could like you in exactly the way you wanted to be liked, could I like you like that? Can you tell me for sure that I am not failing you? If I were failing you, could you tell me how to stop?

But Ed was talking with Anni about that Sunday's choir rehearsal—Larkin had forgotten, until that moment, that the Pratincola Concert Choir was about to end its winter break—and after listening to Ed make a joke about *springing into action* and listening to Anni make a joke about *spring still being six weeks away*, she was glad she hadn't made the moment about herself.

Because that's what she would have done, if she had stopped Ed to ask him what was going on. Even when she tried to make things about other people, it all came right back around to *her*. Larkin looked around the lobby and asked herself if there was anything she could do to help anyone else. Bonnie had what she wanted, thanks to Elliott. Anni had what she wanted, thanks to Elliott. Ed was off-limits, and not just because he had already left for the locker room. That left —and as Bonnie went to set up her class and Anni went to hang up her coat, Larkin looked at the rangy ginger who had once been a magician. She wasn't quite sure *what Elliott wanted*, but she was pretty sure how to start the conversation.

"Thank you," she said.

"You're welcome," he said. "I guess I have to wait here until Bonnie's class is over so I can get my laptop back."

Now Larkin was pretty sure how she could help. "Could I treat you to a coconut water or a protein smoothie?"

"You're not going to class?"

"I'll go next time," Larkin said. "Right now I think I owe you a nutritionally optimized beverage."

The two of them made their way to the fitness center

canteen, where Elliott ordered a bottle of water and Larkin ordered a Drink. She figured she ought to do her bit to support Bonnie, especially since she hadn't done much to help the case so far.

"Aren't you worried about missing a clue?" Elliott asked, as the two of them took their drinks to a metal table.

"I feel like I need to get a clue first," Larkin said. She unscrewed the cap of her Drink and took a tentative swallow. "Wow, this is surprisingly *not terrible*," she said. "It's like a liquid gummy vitamin." She helped herself to a second swig. "I can see why Bonnie was so excited about getting them as a sponsor."

"What do you mean, as a sponsor?"

Larkin explained the situation, as well as she understood it. Then she explained the problem. "Since Bonnie can't post to social media, she might lose her Drink money. That's a significant part of her income, or at least that's what she made it sound like." She took one last drink and placed the empty bottle on the table. "I'm not sure how Bonnie gets paid, exactly. I should have asked. I'm going to ask. You know that Anni just emailed me—I mean, you know everything, I'm not going to explain it to you because I'm not going to talk about me."

Elliott nodded. He did that a lot. Larkin kept talking.

"If I were to guess how Bonnie got paid, well—she's probably getting a little bit from the fitness center and a little bit from the company that provides the music and routines. The fitness center pays the company, and the company provides the fitness center with credibility. Like, *if you take this class you can burn up to 600 calories per hour,* or whatever. But Bonnie also has to provide credibility. That's why she has to be on social media all the time. She's the proof that this whole system works. Without her, it all falls apart."

Larkin pulled at the wrapper of her Drink until it fell apart. Then she shoved the crumpled plastic into the pocket of her mother's coat and took out her phone. "Bonnie's really good at what she does, too. There was this picture she took of Ed that got, like, four thousand likes." She did a search for *Ed Jackson Pratincola fitness.* Maybe she could find the image on an account that hadn't been murdered.

The search engine was unable to find a precise match for Larkin's query—so it began retrieving other Pratincola fitness center posts instead. "Wow," Larkin said, "a lot of people in this town spend a lot of time posting fitness selfies."

"The Eastern Iowa Creative Corridor is one of the healthiest areas in the nation," Elliott said.

"Did Anni tell you that?" Larkin asked. "She said the same thing to me after I moved here. I guess I ended up staying, so it must have worked." She set a second set of search parameters: *Pratincola fitness Bonnie Cooper.* "Sorry, I didn't mean to assume you were staying here too. That was probably rude of me. I haven't slept."

"We haven't decided where we're going to live," Elliott said. "We're pretty sure it's not going to be Anni's apartment."

Larkin was pretty sure Anni would have wanted her to ask Elliott about that—it was a pretty big thing to say, after all—but she was too busy asking the search engine to pull all of the *Pratincola fitness Bonnie Cooper* posts, as well as any posts that included *Pratincola guided fitness* or *Blithe and Bonnie,* that had been made on the day of Bonnie's social media murder. "We might not need the security cameras," Larkin said. "Look at this."

She turned her phone towards Elliott just long enough for him to see the search results. "There are fifty-two posts from the day Bonnie's accounts were killed."

"Not from Bonnie."

"No," Larkin said. "Her accounts are dead. These are all of the posts made by *other people*." She began scrolling. "Nearly all of them have images. Some of them are from *inside the classroom*, where we couldn't even get security camera footage anyway."

"Ha," Larkin said, "there I am. In the background. That was when Bonnie was talking to Anni and me about how we should start a true crime podcast." She showed the image to Elliott.

"I am the luckiest man in the world," Elliott said.

"Why?"

"Because I found Anni again. Because we found each other." He handed the phone back. "Also, that picture has two Bonnies in it."

"Wait, what?" Larkin looked, and Elliott was right— there was the Bonnie who was talking to Larkin and Anni about true crime, and a second, identically dressed Bonnie who appeared to be walking towards the corner of the classroom. The second Bonnie was blurred, and expanding the image didn't make it any clearer.

"Could it be a double exposure or something?"

"That's film," Elliott said.

"What if it was, like, a new social media filter?" Larkin did a quick search for *double exposure filter*—they did exist, but there wasn't any reason for this social media selfie to be doubly exposed. The subject was exposed enough, wearing ill-fitting fitness togs and telling her followers that she was still keeping up with her New Year's Resolution.

"I don't remember our class having two Bonnies in it," Larkin said. "We would have noticed."

"No," Elliott said, "you wouldn't have. It's a classic example of misdirection."

"Thanks, Mister Magician," Larkin said, and Elliott looked just uncomfortable enough that she wished she hadn't. "Sorry. I mean—you think somebody did this deliberately?"

"If somebody did this," Elliott said, "it was deliberate." He examined the photo again. "I suppose it could just be someone who looks a lot like Bonnie, who just happened to be wearing the same clothes."

"Yeah," Larkin said, "she's kind of a type. Especially for Pratincola. There are more natural blondes in Eastern Iowa than there are in the entire state of California." She took her phone back and began searching for other photos with two Bonnies in them. "I saw someone a few hours ago, and I almost called the person Bonnie." That wasn't quite true. "I mean, I actually said *hey, Bonnie*, and they turned around and it wasn't her at all."

Larkin waited for Elliott to respond. Then she remembered Anni's advice. "Do you know what's funny? I lived in Los Angeles when I went to grad school. Ed lived in Los Angeles when he went to grad school. You must have been in Los Angeles at around the same time, when you were doing your TV show. We were probably within a few miles of each other, all three of us, and we all ended up here." She glanced up from her phone to see if Elliott had registered that she was trying to ask him a question. Then she realized she actually hadn't. "I mean, isn't that interesting?"

"In what way do you think it's interesting? I have a couple of theories, but I'd be interested in hearing yours first." Elliott was *way better at asking people questions*. Larkin wondered if that was one of the reasons why Anni liked him.

"I guess I never thought I'd end up in a place like this, and I never thought someone like Ed would end up in a place like this," Larkin said. "I don't know a lot about you yet, but I bet you never wanted to end up in a place like this."

"Ah," Elliott said. "That's not why I think it's interesting."

"Why do you think it's interesting?"

"I think it's interesting because it's completely predictable," Elliott said. "Of course people like you and me and Ed would end up in Pratincola, if that's the way you want to put it." He pulled his phone out of his pocket. "People go where the opportunities are, and right now there are more opportunities in Eastern Iowa than there are in the entire state of California."

Larkin watched Elliott send a text. He used the same two-finger technique that she had seen Anni use—short-long, long-short, long-short, short-short—and she suddenly realized what it was.

"You're texting in Morse code!" she said. "I've been watching Anni tap at her phone for *months*. I wanted to say something, but I thought it would be rude, you aren't supposed to ask people what they're doing on their phones, it's like whenever anyone's texting or emailing or taking a selfie you have to, like, *pretend like they don't exist*, and all this time she was just waiting for me to ask her about it."

"I know," Elliott said, smiling. "I heard the whole story last night."

"So did I," Larkin said.

"Good good good good good!" It was Anni, workout bag in one hand and Elliott's laptop in the other. "I was hoping the two of you would be friends!" She kissed the top of Elliott's head in a way that suggested she would have kissed whatever part of his body was available without worrying about what it meant. "Bonnie's class went well," she continued. "She's going to come up and thank you in a minute, I think."

"Look at this," Larkin said, holding her phone towards Anni. She was about to tell Anni what she and Elliott had found, and then she decided to turn it into a question. "What do you see in this photo?"

"That's Beth," Anni said. "I was helping her out on Monday. Bonnie's class is her New Year's Resolution."

"What else do you see?"

"It must have been taken at the beginning of class," Anni said. "You and I are in the background, with Bonnie, and—"

Larkin watched Anni figure it out. "There's someone else in this photo wearing Bonnie's clothing." She handed the phone back to Larkin. "Not literally Bonnie's clothing."

"Obviously," Larkin said.

"Not obviously," Anni said. "I mean, I know what you meant, but the whole point is that it wasn't supposed to be obvious. Beth didn't notice when she took the selfie. Nobody said anything about it in the comments. We didn't even notice it *when it happened*."

"It's called the Gorilla Effect, right?" Elliott asked.

"Invisible Gorilla," Anni said, "but yes. We see what we expect to see, and because of that, nobody saw this."

"Well," Larkin said, "I guess we need to find out who the Invisible Gorilla is." She stood up, ready to take the next step—and then sat down again. "But maybe tomorrow? I am kind of exhausted, and it's late—"

"It's 5:02," Anni said.

"And I should really check in on my mom, and—"

"What's going on with your mom?" Anni again; Larkin

could see the worst-case scenarios work their way through her imagination.

"Nothing serious," Larkin said, trying to reassure Anni without breaking the unspoken rule to *not tell anyone else about the signs.* "It's a Howell thing. Work stress. She asked me not to talk about it."

"All right," Anni said. "Then we'll leave you to it—oh, hello!" It was Bonnie, finished with her post-workout routine; she slung one arm around Anni and another arm around Larkin and said "Thank you."

"Happy to help," Larkin said. "Although Elliott did most of the work."

"We worked together," Elliott said.

"And if you were interested in getting together tomorrow," Larkin continued, "I might have a lead on your case. Do you want to meet at The Coffee Shop again, maybe around 1 p.m.? That's when my shift's over."

"Sure," Bonnie said, and they settled it, and the four of them made small talk as they made their way out of the fitness center and towards their respective cars and sidewalks. Larkin went home; she asked her mom all the right questions about how her day had gone (well) and whether there had been any new signs (no) and whether Ghoti had set up that appointment (well, *no*), and then she had her dinner and took her shower and watched the first thirteen minutes of a bootleg recording of the latest *Into the Woods* revival before falling asleep.

She woke up, a few minutes after midnight, with one question in her mind:

Why hadn't Ed joined them after class?

CHAPTER 13

Larkin made it to The Coffee Shop on time—
though just barely—and scooped, poured,
dripped, and pulled her way through a second
sleep-deprived shift. It felt like the third day of Tech Week,
which meant it felt familiar; but Tech Week had been easier
to bear, somehow. Doing theater was easier than doing
anything else, which was probably why so many people
tried to do it for a living. It was also something she missed,
in a way she couldn't even have articulated if she had been
awake enough to form coherent sentences. It had given her
life a cohesive structure; a series of cues to follow, lines to
say, directions to give or take.

Not that being a barista was all that different from
being an assistant director—or an actor, for that matter.
Roles were roles were roles, to misquote that poet whose
name Larkin couldn't remember. She wasn't even sure the
woman had been a poet. All she could remember was *Alice
B. Toklas*, which wasn't the right name but was still pretty
sweet. Was that a pun, or just a terrible Shakespearean
reference? Her mother would know. She'd know the name

of the poet, too, and that would give them something to talk about besides *sign* and *resign*. The point was—what was the point? The pun, if it had in fact been one. *Roles, roles, roles*, to misquote Shakespeare for a second time. The duties she'd had in the theater were similar enough to the duties she had as a barista, and if she'd been happier in the theater than she was in The Coffee Shop it had been because theater people always always, *always* treated their work as if it were the only thing that mattered, which meant that every time Larkin was working a show, she hadn't had to worry about anything else that might otherwise have mattered.

Like her love life.

Or whether she knew how to be a good friend.

Or whether she could solve Bonnie's murder.

Why hadn't Ed joined them after class?

Bonnie arrived promptly at 1:00, and when the two of them took their seats at Larkin's preferred corner table— good for interrogating, terrible for every other form of conversation—she immediately showed Bonnie the photo.

"Are you sure?" Bonnie handed the phone back. "I don't see it."

"There's a person wearing the exact same outfit as you," Larkin said. "They could have walked right into class and messed with your phone and nobody would have noticed."

"No," Bonnie said. She crossed her arms across her Drink-branded hoodie. "Nope, nope, nope."

"Wait, what?" Larkin had expected Bonnie to be excited at the prospect of pursuing the person who had inserted themselves into her class to delete her accounts. "This is, like, a *solid lead*."

"I maybe don't need one anymore," Bonnie said. "I can run my class off Elliott's laptop until I set up a new account on my phone, which I could maybe do today." Her left hand twiddled the aglet on her Drink-branded hoodie drawstring. "Yeah. I should do that. Just start over or something." She pulled the string, drawing half of the hood towards her left shoulder. "Or maybe do something completely different. I don't know."

She looked, in that moment, nothing like the Bonnie Cooper whom Larkin had come to know. Nothing like either Bonnie Cooper, really; both the likeable social media personality and the person with the asymmetric smile had been replaced by a woman with narrow eyes and a wrinkled brow and a frown that was slightly wider on the left-hand side.

Possibly because that was where Bonnie had placed her aglet.

To chew it.

Larkin got up and got Bonnie a cup of Coffee Shop water. Bonnie removed her drawstring just long enough to take a sip; then she popped the aglet back into her mouth and continued to ruminate. The part of Larkin that knew she was supposed to be either an amateur or professional detective also knew that she should be drawing some kind of conclusion—or at least some kind of *clue*—from all of this, but the part of Larkin that was always aware of what her phone was doing had just noticed a new text message.

From Ed.

Hey! Your shift just ended, right? Want to get lunch? Or, if you've already had lunch, coffee?

Bonnie, who had gotten all of the nutrition that was available from her Drink-branded clothing, stood up and said "I should get going."

"Wait," Larkin said. She put her phone face-down on the table. "We should talk." This was, of course, what she wanted to text Ed—but that could wait, especially because

Larkin hadn't yet decided what to say. She hadn't really decided what to say to Bonnie, either—but there was one question that always worked, especially if people were willing to answer it honestly.

"What do you want?"

"To be done with this." Bonnie's statement could be taken as both text and subtext; objective and superobjective were both stated and both—Larkin immediately understood—*meant*.

"So are you going to quit your job?"

"It isn't really a job," Bonnie said. "If it were, people would take it seriously."

"What if I told you that I took it seriously?" Larkin hadn't been sure, until that moment, whether she did in fact take Bonnie's job seriously. She hadn't even been sure that she would have called it a *job*. But she made a choice, as all good scene partners should, and waited to see how Bonnie would respond.

"I don't know," Bonnie said. "It's not, like, what you do."

"Being a detective?"

"No," Bonnie said. "Working *here*. You have, like, a regular paycheck. Based on hours, so you always know what it's going to be. It's a real job."

Larkin hadn't been sure that she would have called her Coffee Shop gig a *real job*. It was a job, to be sure, and one she was glad to have—but it wasn't what she really wanted to do, so she had avoided thinking of it in any terms that weren't temporary.

On the other hand, she still didn't know what she really wanted to do—but now was *not the time for that*.

"You also have time when you're, like, *not working*," Bonnie continued. "I bet you got Christmas off."

"Yep," Larkin said. "Christmas to New Year's." This

had been a burden as much as it had been a benefit; Larkin had missed out on a week of earning money, and she had spent much of the week wondering whether Ed missed her. Now she wondered if he was wondering why she hadn't replied to his text—but it wasn't the time for that either. "Didn't the fitness center close too?"

"Yeah," Bonnie said, "but I was still making content. Every day." She sat down again. "I don't think my family liked that very much."

"Why not?"

"I don't want to talk about it."

This, Larkin immediately understood, meant it was *the one thing she needed to get Bonnie to talk about*. "My Christmas wasn't what I was hoping it would be either," she said, hoping that she was making the right choice. "You know Ed, right?"

"Everyone knows Ed."

"Right." Larkin thought about the best way to say what needed to be said. "Well, he had invited me to Thanksgiving dinner with his family, and I thought for sure we'd be spending Christmas together, but he never asked."

"Did you ask?"

"No," Larkin said. "You can't ask someone to invite you to their family's Christmas celebration."

"But you could have asked him to yours."

"It wasn't mine, though," Larkin said. "It was my mom's and her new girlfriend's. I was just there as, like, the weird adult daughter who lives in the guest bedroom." Larkin knew that wasn't true as soon as she said it. She wasn't sure why she hadn't known it wasn't true before.

"And I was just, like, the weird sister who has this career that nobody understands," Bonnie said. "It's like they didn't even care that I had just gotten my first major sponsor. They didn't care that I could earn a bonus if my

posts were in the top ten percent of the company dashboard. All they wanted was for me to put my phone
away."

"Did you?"

"No," Bonnie said. "I got the bonus."

"And then you got murdered," Larkin said.

"Yes," Bonnie said.

"Do you know who did it?"

Larkin watched Bonnie decide whether or not to tell
the truth. "It doesn't matter."

"Of course it matters," Larkin said. "What you do
matters. The fact that you got a nutrition solution to give
you money to say good things about its product matters.
The fact that you got me to, like, *agree to do lunges three
times a week* matters. Beth is sticking to her New Year's
Resolution because of you. The Pratincola fitness center
only exists because of people like you."

"That's not true," Bonnie said. "It would exist
otherwise."

"Yeah, as a track and a room with a bunch of free
weights," Larkin said. "We need the classes. We need you,
Bonnie Cooper."

She watched Bonnie decide whether any of this was
true. "So you're saying I should become un-murdered."

"Only if you want to."

"I don't know." Bonnie stood up a second time. "I
should go."

This time, Larkin didn't say *wait*. Instead, she waited
for Bonnie to leave—and then she followed her.

———

Bonnie was as easy to follow as Anni had been, especially
once Larkin figured out where she was headed. Larkin

parked her car a few blocks away from Howell College, then picked her way carefully across uneven, unsalted sidewalk towards the apartment complex where Bonnie lived.

The cluster of dilapidated terraces was not as easy to navigate as Anni's apartment building, but—luckily for Larkin—Bonnie's section was far enough away from the parking lot that Larkin was able to spot her before she went inside. Larkin bisected a central gathering place, passing from grass to cement and back again, noting the wet leaves and red plastic cups that had gathered at the bottom of the empty swimming pool. It was easy to tell, from the state of the terraces, which tenants viewed their current state as temporary. Bonnie's terrace currently sported a set of pink dumbbells and a pair of Howell-branded lawn chairs. There were also twin wind chimes, one on each side of the sliding screen doors.

Larkin did not want to get close enough to be seen, but she knew how sightlines worked—as long as she was unable to see into Bonnie's apartment, nobody inside would be able to see her. Sound traveled a little differently, so she stepped quickly and quietly towards the non-windowed wall. This was probably trespassing, but she could always say she was just passing through. It wouldn't be her fault if she heard something. It would be the land-lord's fault, for allowing tenants to rent a place with substandard insulation.

So she listened.

"I had lunch with Dad. He wants to know if we're going to be at church tomorrow."

"What did he really want to know?" That was Bonnie. The other voice was not.

"I don't know," the voice that wasn't Bonnie said. "You know Dad."

There was a noise—a phone, pinging—and a pause.

"That was Mom," not-Bonnie said. "I'll tell her to tell Dad we'll be at church."

"And lunch afterwards?"

"That's the whole point of church," not-Bonnie said. "Honor thy father and mother, get a free lunch. Make it through the entire lunch without taking the Lord's name in vain, and they'll slip you a twenty afterwards."

Larkin wondered what her mother would think of that arrangement. Josephine would probably object to the psychology first and the theology second, arguing that neither the preaching nor the practice yielded adults who were capable of navigating the world without coveting their parents' twenty-dollar bills.

"I'm going to tell them you said that," Bonnie said.

"You had better not," not-Bonnie said. "I'm the good one, remember?"

"Only because you do whatever Daddy tells you to do."

"He doesn't ask much," not-Bonnie said. "And we get a lot in return."

Another pause. The hum of a microwave.

"I taught my class today," Bonnie said. "Even though my accounts were gone. I was able to contact customer service and they let me on my dashboard."

"How'd you get on your phone?"

"I didn't," Bonnie said. "I borrowed someone else's laptop."

"Huh," not-Bonnie said. "I guess that could work."

"Yeah," Bonnie said. "It totally worked. I'm going to keep doing it until I get my new accounts set up, I may have to make all new logins and I may lose all my emails but *whatever*, and then I'm going to figure out how to contact customer service to get *Blithe and Bonnie* back."

The microwave dinged; the microwave door was punched open.

"What if I said you couldn't?"

"What do you mean?"

"That was our account," not-Bonnie said. "What if I said I didn't want you to keep using it?"

"Why would you do that?"

"Because maybe I don't want to be associated with your *content*."

"You aren't associated! At all! People would have to scroll back, like, *seven years* to find the stuff we did together!"

"I don't care," not-Bonnie said, "My face, my name, my consent."

"It's not even spelled the same way!"

"But everyone who knows you knows me," not-Bonnie said. "We've been a package deal ever since we were born."

"Maybe in Pratincola," Bonnie said, "but none of my followers even know I have a twin sister! I never, ever, *ever* mention it. In *Blithe and Bonnie* world, *you don't exist.*"

"Well, maybe I'm tired of not existing."

"You're always tired of something, Blythe!"

A door slammed. Larkin waited, wondering if she needed to flatten herself against the ground or something —but Bonnie walked back to her car without looking to see if the amateur private detective she hired was hiding next to the chipped-paint siding of her apartment build-ing. Larkin watched Bonnie drive away, and was about to follow her when she heard a second set of footsteps. Blythe, this time. Same height, same hair, but not at all the same person—and yet strangely familiar, even when all Larkin could see was a blonde ponytail caught in the hood of a blue puffer coat.

Larkin watched Blythe unlock her own car. The two SUVs shared both make and model; gifts, presumably, from their parents. Bonnie's vehicle was as clean as the day it left the lot; Blythe's bumper was splattered with mud and her driver-side mirror was held on by duct tape. She did not see Larkin, even though the sightlines would have made it very, very easy. Both twins had left the apartment without looking back.

This meant that Larkin had to wait for Blythe's car to turn out of the parking lot before she could catch a glimpse of her face—and once she did, she knew exactly where she'd seen Blythe before.

———

Larkin's first stop was the campus bookstore. Her second stop was Ghoti's social media feed. Her third stop was the Howell library.

Larkin's mother had told her all about the renovation —*recent*, if the word were allowed to encompass *the past decade*—and so Larkin knew not to expect the library to contain any visible books. "Our students use the Howell app to request the texts they need," her mother had said, "and our student-leader librarians retrieve them." Dean Day had not initially been in favor of removing the stacks; she had argued that there was an advantage in allowing students to explore the books on their own, discovering subjects and authors they might never have otherwise considered. Unfortunately, enough Howell students were using the stacks for purposes she had not initially considered—many of which involved *exploration*, few of which involved *books*—that the Howell administration had unanimously agreed to disallow access.

"There's much less theft, that's for sure," her mother

had said, "and many fewer misshelvings."

There were also many more opportunities for Howell to make money—the library included both a café and an arcade, as well as several pay-by-the-hour study carrels. Students who could not afford a soundproofed study pod were invited to lounge on one of the many oversized, primary-colored sofas and chairs, each of which was outfitted with its own multi-outlet charger. There were a series of affinity rooms with unique designations and design schemes. Larkin had expected to find Ghoti in the Gender Nonconforming room, but Ghoti had chosen to non-conform by squishing themselves into the one space no student would voluntarily go—in the corner, on the floor, next to the two long-unused drinking fountains.

"Is Blythe Cooper your boss?"

"Yes." Ghoti looked up. "Why are you here?"

"Because I can always find the information I'm looking for at the library," Larkin said.

"Fair enough." Ghoti pushed their hair out of their eyes. "Want to sit down?"

Larkin did not—she knew Howell was in the business of cutting costs, and the state of the carpet suggested they were also in the business of cutting corners—but she did anyway. Ghoti, as she expected, did not smell particularly *fresh*.

"Want a gummy worm?" Ghoti reached into their bag and retrieved a smaller bag full of pink-and-yellow worms; after pulling unsuccessfully at the seam, they took their pen and punctured a hole in the plastic. A pinky finger followed, pushing its way in and hooking itself around a worm.

"Do you eat those on purpose?"

"Does anybody eat anything by accident?"

Larkin thought of her last—or, if she was really going

to pursue this career, *first*—murder case. "Sometimes people aren't aware of what they're consuming," she said, not wanting to explain how she knew what she was talking about. "Or maybe they aren't aware of how it reads"—the theatrical term was out of her mouth before she knew what she was saying—"to other people."

"I am aware of both the nutritional and the semiotic value," Ghoti said, pulling another worm out of the pouch.

"You really need to set up that meeting with my mom," Larkin said. "She would love you."

"And Janessa would hate setting it up," Ghoti said. "It would almost be worth it."

"What's your deal with Janessa?"

Ghoti sucked sugar off their pinky. "Detectives only ask questions when they already know the answers, right?"

"I think those are lawyers," Larkin said. She made a mental note to check the Iowa Association of Private Investigators website later, just to make sure. "So you're saying I should already know why you dislike Janessa?"

"I didn't say I disliked her," Ghoti said.

"You're right," Larkin said. "You said she would hate setting up the meeting."

"Because?" Ghoti was eating their third worm in segments.

"Because she hates her job."

"Everyone hates their jobs."

"Because she doesn't want you to meet my mother."

"She would love for me to meet your mother." Ghoti stretched the last bit of worm between their fingers. "Not by invitation, though."

"Because—"

"Come on," Ghoti said. "I said I didn't say *I disliked her*."

"Because she doesn't like you."

"Got it," Ghoti said, dropping the gummy into their mouth.

Larkin couldn't decide whether to explain to Ghoti why they might be, for lack of a better term, *dislikable*, or to refrain from any further discussion. The second option would, at least, get her off the carpet—but then she remembered why she had called on Ghoti in the first place.

"What about Blythe?" she asked. "She sounds like someone you might dislike."

"Blythe hates herself too much to care whether I like her or not," Ghoti said.

"But you do," Larkin said. "I mean, you don't." She leaned her head against the library wall and tried not to think about how many hours stood between her and sleep. "You don't like her."

"It doesn't matter," Ghoti said.

Larkin had heard that somewhere before. She couldn't remember. She wondered if Ghoti would notice if she closed her eyes. She figured Ghoti was one of those people who noticed everything. She wondered if she should introduce Ghoti to Anni. The two of them could notice things, back and forth, forever. She'd heard that somewhere before, too.

"Hey," Ghoti said. "Wake up. I'll show you something."

They tapped at their laptop until a video appeared. Not a recent video—it was horizontal, and slightly blurred— but maybe a decade old. Two girls, both blondes, dressed in nearly identical outfits. Their faces were also nearly identical; the only difference was that the girl in pink was pretty and the girl in blue wasn't.

"Welcome to another episode of Blithe and Bonnie!" It was the girl in blue who said it. Larkin would have expected Bonnie to be running the show. Instead, she watched as Blythe urged everyone watching to like and subscribe. "With your help, we can get to 500 followers by Christmas!"

The two of them used the next four minutes of video to chat about their holiday plans—"we're going ice skating!" —and share the seven best ways to wrap a present. Blythe kept up the patter while Bonnie cut the paper; she smiled, delicately and asymmetrically, as she held up her first wrapped box. "You can use a creasing stick," she said, "but if you don't have one, that's okay. A butter knife will work, or even your fingernail."

Bonnie offered this advice as a gift; Blythe took it away by adding "If you liked that tip, ring that bell! Give a pair of holiday angels their wings!"

Ghoti paused the video. "So, yeah. That's Blythe. Before she removed every reference to her old self." They pulled another worm out of the plastic bag. "I guess she thinks her new self is better, or something."

"Something like that," Larkin said. She wasn't sure if she should tell Ghoti that their guess was incorrect, or if that would be betraying some kind of detective-client privilege. One more thing to add to the list of things she'd look up later. "Why do you have this?"

"I figured someone should save it," Ghoti said. "People think that deleting something from the internet makes it, like, *disappear*." They smudged a thumb across their laptop screen; the two blonde girls vanished. "But there are always ways to make copies."

"How much did you copy?"

"Pretty much everything," Ghoti said.

"Why?"

"Because I heard Blythe, on her break, tell her dad that she was going to delete all of her old social media accounts." Ghoti picked at a bit of the carpet. "So I started downloading stuff. It only took a few hours. Mostly I wanted to see if I could do it."

"Does Blythe know?"

"No," Ghoti said. "She thinks they're gone for good."

No, Larkin thought, *she thinks they're gone for bad.*

She almost made the quip aloud—she would have, if she'd been able to decide whether it was in fact *a pun*—but Ghoti was packing up and standing up and putting the half-eaten bag of gummy worms into their pocket. "I hope you got what you were looking for," they said. "Tell your mom I'll set up the meeting on Monday."

———

Larkin did in fact relay the information to her mother, before laying herself down on the couch and falling asleep in front of what would have been the television if they had had one. She woke up several hours later; someone had tucked a blanket around her, and there was a sticky note hanging off her mother's booklight: *We went to bed. So did you! Love your mom and Claire.*

It was obvious that Claire had written the note; the handwriting was the first clue, and the presence of an exclamation point and absence of a comma suggested her mother had neither written nor proofread. The house was dark, besides the booklight; Pal was keeping watch in the kitchen doorway. When Larkin tapped at her phone to see what time it was, she saw Ed's unanswered text message.

Hey! Your shift just ended, right? Want to get lunch? Or, if you've already had lunch, coffee?

She had left Ed on read, which was bad enough.

What was worse was that she had completely forgotten about him.

CHAPTER 14

The first person Larkin texted, the next morning, was Anni.

What if I needed your help for a personal thing
Would you be free or whatever

She didn't get the response until 1:15.

sorry, was out with Elliott
still am in fact
is everything okay?

Larkin knew that she could probably pull Anni's attention away from Elliott if she demanded it; she also knew that she didn't want to. If Anni had texted back in time for Larkin to ask for advice and then invite Ed to lunch (or, if he'd already had lunch, coffee), it would have been one thing; at this point, it wasn't worth losing friend points with Anni to try to gain girlfriend points with Ed.

Yes, all is fine, don't worry
Have fun with your Fox
See you at choir rehearsal?

This time the response came immediately.

yes

The rehearsal began at 2. Larkin wanted to arrive early enough to talk to Anni but not so early that she'd have to have an uncomfortable conversation with Ed; she sat in the parking lot for ten minutes watching cars pull in, only to realize that Anni must have arrived, on foot, at least fifteen minutes ago.

Which meant that Larkin was, once again, late to choir rehearsal.

She hadn't been late to any of the previous Pratincola choral rehearsals, not since she and Ed had started dating or sort-of-dating or whatever-it-is-they-were-doing. She had been late to rehearsal before, though. Back when Ed was directing the megachoir, and they were preparing to sing Beethoven's Ninth in Cedar Rapids and Iowa City with the Corridorchestra. Back when she and Ed weren't a thing. She wondered if he would remember; if he would evaluate her arrival status and re-evaluate their relationship status.

Instead, Ed smiled.

"Sorry," Larkin mouthed, taking her seat among the altos. Anni was at the piano. Elliott was with the baritones —she'd have expected him to be a tenor, but she never guessed vocal ranges correctly—and was sharing music with Ben, who was very, very aware that the left half of his folder was being held by someone who had once hosted his own television show. Larkin knew, of course, because of the way Ben raised his eyebrows after catching her eye. Not that Ben would be weird about it or anything; his partner, Mitchell, was noteworthy in his own right, which meant that Ben would spend rehearsal helping Elliott through the right notes, and save any questions of notoriety for the dinners he and Mitchell regularly hosted.

Larkin wondered if she would still be invited to those dinners, if she and Ed broke up.

The music they were singing—and Larkin had looked at her music in advance, this time—was all about love. Red, red roses and pleasant groves, *happy, happy, happy, happy*—and she had been, the first time she'd opened her folder and perused the Purcell. She'd been delighted, when the choral secretary had handed out the spring concert selections before they broke for the winter holidays. She knew that choirs sang about love pretty much every time they weren't singing about death, but it still felt like Ed had chosen all of this music just for her.

Just for *them*, it would have been.

Is that why it wasn't, now? Had she missed the *them* part of her and Ed, just like she'd missed the *friend* part of her and Anni?

But Anni, at the break, appeared to have both forgiven and forgotten. "What did you want to talk about? We could go back to my apartment after rehearsal if you wanted. Elliott will be there, since that's where all of his stuff is, but we can ask him to be somewhere else."

Elliott, at that moment, had disappeared—"he is even worse at small talk than I am," Anni explained—and Ed appeared to be giving a moment of his time to each Pratincola choral singer, asking how vacations had gone and how back-to-school was going and everything else you had to talk about when it was too soon to talk about corn.

This meant that Larkin could talk about Ed, as long as she kept it *sotto voce*. "I may have screwed things up with our conductor," she said. "Big-time."

"What did you do?" Anni looked concernedly at Ed, then at Larkin. Larkin stepped between Ed and Anni so that he could neither see her face nor read either of their lips. Not that she knew whether Ed could read lips, of course. It was one of the many things she didn't know about him.

"I forgot to reply to a text."

Now Anni looked confused. "Is that a big-time screw-up?"

"He was asking me"—and Larkin dropped her voice to the quietest of whispers—"*to lunch.*"

Anni furrowed her forehead. "I don't see the problem." She squinted her eyes closed. "I'm trying very hard to see it." She opened them again. "Okay, so you missed the chance to have lunch with Ed. And you feel badly because you think he thinks you forgot about him."

"I did forget about him!" Larkin said. "I'm a terrible girlfriend!"

"First of all," Anni said, "there is no way you can connect those two statements."

"They are *obviously connected,*" Larkin said.

"No," Anni said, "you don't understand. Mathematically, there is no way to prove that your two premises yield any logical conclusion. It's a classic cognitive fallacy that I can't remember the name of right now, and when I tell Elliott about it later he isn't going to say that makes me a bad girlfriend."

"Well, what I forgot was more important," Larkin said.

"It was lunch," Anni said. "It comes around once a day."

"No," Larkin said. "I didn't forget *lunch.* I forgot *Ed.*"

She had also forgotten to keep track of where Ed was, in the room—which is why she flinched when he placed his hand on her shoulder.

"Hey," Ed said. "How are things going?"

"I'm so sorry I forgot to respond to your text the other

day," Larkin said. "I was with Bonnie Cooper, you know Bonnie, of course you know Bonnie, and then I kind of followed her and discovered that she has a twin, did you know she has a twin, and then I had this conversation with Ghoti, you know, G-h-o-t-i, we talked about them the last time we went to lunch, you remember, of course you remember, and I should have let you know what was going on."

"No worries," Ed said. "You sound pretty busy."

"How are you doing?" Anni asked Ed—and Larkin suddenly realized that if she had thought, *at all*, about how Ed was doing, she could have been the one to ask it.

"Well, I don't know if I'm as busy as Larkin," Ed said, "but you'll be happy to know that I sent off all my documentation this morning."

"Congratulations!" Anni said. "So now all you have to do is wait, right?"

"And teach," Ed said, "and lead the Pratincola Concert Choir, and prepare this piece that they've asked me to sing with the orchestra in Cedar Rapids, and get ready to musical-direct Summer Shakespeare."

"They're doing Summer Shakespeare again?" This was another question that Anni had known to ask instead of Larkin.

"Yeah," Ed said, "they're bringing it back. Four weeks of rehearsal, two weekends of *Romeo and Juliet*."

"Generously sponsored, in part, by my better half." It was Ben, joining the three of them by the piano. "Anni," he said. "*Scarbo*?"

"Not anymore," Anni said, "and please don't ask him about it."

"I would *never*," Ben said. "I mean, now that you've told me not to." He smiled at Larkin. "Mitchell wants to know when you're going to come by the house again. He's very interested in your thoughts on the latest revisions to my opera. Ed, we'll have you too if you're not doing tenure stuff, I'll get a Bordeaux for you and Champagne for the lady. Anni, what does your adorable ginger friend like to drink?"

"Nearly anything," Anni said. "Just make sure it doesn't say *magic* on the bottle, or *illusion*, or—"

"Or *television series cancellation*," Ben said. "I get it."

"We should get back to rehearsal," Ed said. "Tell Mitchell that I'll be a maybe on whatever you're planning."

"What if we only planned it for a day when we knew you'd be a *yes*?"

But Ed didn't have time to answer Ben's question—not that Ben would have accepted any answer that suggested Ed didn't have time—and Larkin didn't have time to ask any of the questions she should have asked.

Or, more accurately, *should have been asking*.

Was Ed up for tenure this year? Was that why her mother had said he was busy? Were those the documents he was putting together, or were those other kinds of documents? Like—job hunting documents? Was Ed planning on leaving? Is that why he hadn't wanted to spend Christmas with Larkin? But then why would he volunteer to do this Shakespeare thing—and why hadn't he told Larkin that he was doing the music for *Romeo and Juliet*? Why hadn't he asked her what she thought of Shakespeare's most famous play, aside from *Hamlet* and *A Midsummer Night's Dream* and *King Lear* and the one you weren't ever supposed to say out loud? Why hadn't he said anything about any of this to her?

It couldn't be just because she hadn't asked.

That wouldn't be fair.

The songs they sang, in the second half of rehearsal, were all about goodbyes. Roads rising, death approaching, *I wish you peace until we meet again.*

And Larkin sat and sang and wished she knew what to do next.

CHAPTER 15

"Well," Anni said, "why don't you invite him to lunch tomorrow?"

The two of them were in Anni's apartment; Elliott had left without being asked. His suitcase remained, as did two laptops, three decks of cards, and four pocket-sized chess sets. Anni had repositioned her plants to give Elliott enough room to set up the chessboards; now she picked up the board closest to the edge of the table and moved it to the piano bench. Then she gave Larkin coffee and a coaster.

"I should," Larkin said, "but then what should I *say*?"

"Whatever you want," Anni said, "as long as it's true." She carried her own cup of tea to the sofa, sipping it carefully before sitting down. "And not cruel."

"So I should ask him if he's up for tenure this year?"

"Yes," Anni said.

"Wait," Larkin said. "Do you already know whether Ed's up for tenure this year?"

"Yes," Anni said again.

"Why didn't you tell me?"

Anni sipped her tea. "You never asked."

"No," Larkin said. "That isn't how this is going to go. Plenty of people share things about themselves, or things about other people, *without waiting to be asked*. You cannot say this is all my fault for not asking Ed whether he had started to put together his tenure file."

"You're right," Anni said. "It isn't all your fault."

"Do you know how much I hated people asking me how I was doing on the dissertation?" Larkin felt like she needed to clarify, precisely, *why this wasn't her fault*. "It was my least favorite question, next to *how's your love life*." Her coffee was bitter, and too hot; she'd poured the water straight from the boil instead of waiting. "I also hated *how many more years are you going to do the academic job market* and *how much longer are you going to stay in Los Angeles*?"

Anni sipped her tea without comment.

"So you're saying I should have been asking Ed all of those questions?" Larkin tasted her coffee again. Sometimes it tasted better after you'd burnt your mouth. "Not about Los Angeles, obviously, but maybe about how much longer he was going to stay in Pratincola?"

"I don't know," Anni said. "I don't know anything about you and Ed."

"Neither do I!"

"No," Anni said, "you don't know anything about *Ed*. You know a lot about *you-and-Ed*, as a couple. Much more than I do." She cupped her mug between both hands. "I didn't understand this until Elliott, so please understand that I'm telling you something that I've only very recently learned myself."

Larkin watched Anni pause, as she considered exactly how to explain it. "Whenever there are two people," Anni said, "there is a relationship that exists between those two people."

Larkin waited for Anni to continue.

Anni did not.

"Okay," Larkin said. "Whenever there are two people, there is a relationship that exists between those two people."

Anni sipped her tea.

"Everyone knows that," Larkin finally said.

"No, they don't," Anni said. "They're terrible at knowing that."

She stood up, put her empty mug into the sink, and then picked up one of Elliott's decks of cards. "This is the one he says I can touch," Anni said. "The others are for magic."

"I thought he wasn't going to do magic anymore."

"This is a different kind of magic," Anni said. "I'll tell you later. Right now I want you to tell me about the relationship that exists between you and Ed." She sat down again. "I mean, if you don't mind."

"I'm kind of his girlfriend," Larkin said. "Which makes him kind of my boyfriend."

"Kind of." Anni fanned out Elliott's cards, showing the faces to Larkin. They were in order, beginning with the Ace of Hearts and ending with the Ace of Spades. "What is your actual relationship?"

"Boyfriend-girlfriend."

"What does that mean?"

Larkin considered the possible answers. Then she answered honestly. "We spend time together," she said, "when we're both free. I spend the night, sometimes. We talk about stuff, sometimes. Or we watch TV. At least once a week we have lunch at The Coffee Shop."

Anni cut the deck of cards. Then she arranged the two partial decks so that they were perpendicular to each other. "So you're like this," she said, holding the decks out to Larkin. "There's you, and there's Ed, and in between there's lunch and television."

"And sex," Larkin said.

"Well, obviously," Anni said. "Otherwise you'd say you were just good friends." She looked down at the decks in her hand. "But what exists between you that wouldn't exist if the two of you weren't boyfriend and girlfriend?"

"The sex," Larkin said again.

Anni nodded—just as Elliott had, when he and Larkin sat in the Pratincola fitness center canteen. Larkin wondered if Anni had subconsciously adopted the behavior, or if it was deliberate. With Anni, everything was nearly always deliberate. Even now, Larkin could see Anni deliberating what to say next.

"Ask me what exists between me and Elliott."

"What exists between you and Elliott?"

Anni shuffled the deck, letting the cards arc and interlace in a perfect riffle. "We don't know yet," she said. "Not for sure." She held out the shuffled deck to Larkin. "But it's like this. It's an entirely new thing that has never existed before. Not in the *known universe*."

She turned over the top card. Two of hearts. "We're still two separate individuals."

She turned the deck over so Larkin could see the card at the bottom. Ace of hearts. "But we're committed to a single goal."

She fanned the deck out so Larkin could see every card in between. "To learn, together, *what we are*."

Larkin watched as Anni efficiently put the deck back in order. "That's why we didn't work, the first time. I had this idea of what we were going to be, and he had a different idea, and both of us thought that the idea had to come first." She put the deck back on the coffee table. "Like, I thought he was going to be *the magician*, which meant I had to be *the magician's assistant*, and because I didn't want to be that, I didn't even ask myself if there was anything else we could be." She looked at Larkin. "I didn't even ask him."

"Well, he didn't ask you either."

Anni shook her head. "You're missing the point. We could have, and we didn't, because we didn't understand that relationships were something you *made*. We thought relationships were these things you bought into, like an index fund, and if the relationship doesn't follow the growth curve you were hoping for, you transfer your assets to someone else."

Larkin hadn't thought of relationships in quite that way before—but as soon as Anni said it, she wasn't sure she had ever thought of them in any other way.

"So," Anni said again. "What exists between you and Ed?"

"Compared to what exists between you and Elliott?"

"It doesn't have to be compared to anything," Anni said. "But it has to be *something*."

CHAPTER 16

"Remind me again of what you said," Larkin asked her mother.

"What I said?" The two of them were at their usual places in the kitchen, or what had once been their usual places before Larkin got a part-time job that required her to leave the house before dawn four days a week. This was one of the days she got to sleep in, a term that had now been modified to include *waking up at 7 a.m.* —which is how she and her mother ended up making coffee and toast together, just like the old days.

Not that Larkin could justify thinking of the previous summer as *the old days.* But they were, in a sense; Larkin had been new to Pratincola, new to living with her mother, new to Ed and Anni and Claire and Ben and Mitchell and everyone else, new to an entire life that no longer fit the routine she and her mother had once shared.

But today it did—and so Larkin twitched her nose at her mother, reminding her of their other shared routine. "You said there were three things you needed to do to have an important conversation."

"Right," Josephine said, twitching her nose back. "And wrong." Larkin watched her mother push at the toaster lever until the bread popped high enough to pull out. "These are tips to help you have a difficult conversation." She put one of the slices on a plate for Larkin. "All difficult conversations are important, but—"

"Not all important conversations are difficult."

Josephine held up the remaining slice of bread, toasting her daughter. "Well done."

"Well," Larkin said, opening the tub that contained her mother's favorite butter substitute, "let's say this conversation is both important and potentially difficult." She applied just enough not-butter to her bread to cover the burned spots. "And let's say I'm not going to tell you what it is, so don't ask."

"Fine," Josephine said. "Jam?"

"Not if you can help me get out of it," Larkin said, accepting the jar of strawberry preserves and adding just enough to her toast to cover whatever the butter wasn't. "What are the three things?"

"Four things," her mother said. "You decide what you want to say, you stick to what needs to be said, and you say it. Then you listen."

Larkin bit into her toast, leaning over her plate to ensure none of the residue would end up on the table. She was nearly thirty-six years old and she still hadn't figured out how to eat a piece of toast without leaving crumbs—or, in this case, a blob of jam. She couldn't be blamed for not knowing how to have a difficult conversation. "And then after you listen, you decide what to say next, stick to what needs to be said next, et cetera?"

"If you want," Larkin's mother said. "But there's one more thing you need to know."

"A fifth thing?"

"If you want," Larkin's mother said again. "Before you begin a difficult conversation, you need to know when—and how—you're going to end the conversation."

"What do you mean?"

"I mean," Josephine said, "you need to decide both *what you're going to say* and *when you're going to walk away.*"

"What if you don't want to walk away?"

"Then you're not ready to have the conversation."

This was one of the times when Larkin really, really, *really* wanted to ask her mother about her father. Her parents had been married, before Larkin had been old enough to remember them together—which meant that one of them must have started a difficult conversation that ended with one of them walking away.

But Larkin's mother wanted to finish her toast and finish her coffee and get to campus, and so Larkin spent the rest of her morning thinking about what she wanted to say to Ed and whether she was, in fact, ready to say it.

―――――

They met, this time, in the Howell College cafeteria. Larkin knew from experience that she couldn't walk into The Coffee Shop on a day she wasn't working, because then it would become *a day she was working*—and although she needed the money, she needed this meeting with Ed even more.

Not that she should think of it as a meeting. That wasn't the kind of thing you did, with a boyfriend—but what they were doing couldn't really be called a date, not with the plastic chairs and metal trays and the cereal bowl Larkin had filled with honey-colored Os, rainbow-shaped marshmallows, a peeled banana, and chocolate milk.

Ed had a salad.

Larkin began chunking her banana into bits with her spoon. *Decide what you're going to say.* She couldn't ask him, straight out, what existed between them. It was obvious. The two of them went together like salad and cereal. The only thing they had in common was that they had once found a dead body together.

That wasn't true, though. Larkin knew that wasn't true as soon as she thought it. She wasn't sure why she hadn't known it wasn't true before.

"Here's what we have in common," Larkin said, aloud, without deciding what she was going to say first. Her mother wasn't always right about everything. Neither was Anni. Neither was she. "I mean, I should ask you what you think we have in common, but I bet we're going to come up with similar answers."

"Okay," Ed said. He was affable, unflappable, the only person Larkin knew who could eat a salad without ending up with a fork full of lettuce that had to be contorted into an open mouth. Did he cut the lettuce beforehand? Or fold each leaf onto the tines of his fork? She really should pay better attention to her maybe-boyfriend.

"First of all, we're both artists. You more than me, right now, and maybe I was never much of an artist in the practitioner sense, but we're both interested in what art can do." She carried a spoonful of cereal towards her mouth. A chunk of banana fell off and splashed into the milk. "Like, the capacity of art. The ability to connect with people through ideas."

"All right," Ed said. "Although I think you're more of an artist than you realize."

"In what way?"

"In your ability to put things together," Ed said. "You're an excellent director."

"You've never seen me direct."

"Yes, I have," Ed said. "I saw what you did with your mother and Claire, the way you brought them together and got them to trust each other. I see you working with Ben on his opera, nudging him to make it better, helping him understand what connects and what doesn't. I watched you sit next to Anni, during all of those rehearsals for Beethoven's Ninth, and every time the two of you were together she got better at interacting with people."

Ed took another bite of salad. Larkin watched to see if he did anything unusual with his fork. "Also, Ghoti stopped me in the music building the other day to inform me that you were one of the few people in Pratincola worth knowing."

"Well, that makes me sound pretty great," Larkin said, "although I'd take anything Ghoti said with, like, twelve grains of salt."

"And a squeeze of lemon," Ed said.

Larkin smiled. Ed smiled back. He had the tiniest piece of spinach stuck between two of his teeth. "Okay, second of all, we both like the same kinds of jokes," Larkin said. "We're clever, which is fine, you can have a lot of fun being clever, but—"

She was about to say *but it's not enough to build a relationship on*, but decided she didn't really want to say that. Not yet, anyway. Maybe not at all, depending on how Ed responded.

Say what needs to be said.

"Third of all, we're both outsiders."

Larkin watched Ed, to see if he would take this the wrong way. She had made the mistake, early on, of assuming that he hadn't grown up in the Midwest. She wondered if Ed would tell her she had just made another one.

But he watched her, and he read her face if not her

mind, and he finally said "You're right. You and I—for different reasons, of course—don't quite fit in here." He poked his fork into his salad bowl, extracting a piece of lettuce, a sliver of green pepper, and a slice of black olive. "Not yet, anyway."

"And neither of us are sure we want to," Larkin said.

"No," Ed said, after chewing and swallowing his vegetables, "I think I want to."

"Which means you aren't completely sure you want to." Larkin was sure of this. Ed didn't make sense otherwise. She-and-Ed didn't make sense otherwise.

"No," Ed said again. "Pratincola is a good place to live. Howell is a good place to teach. I'm a few hours away from my parents, we're a few miles away from a major regional orchestra, there's always something interesting going on in Cedar Rapids or Iowa City." He smiled again. The spinach was still there. "There are good reasons to want to make this part of the world your home."

"Okay," Larkin said. "But when Anni talks about living in Pratincola, she makes it sound like the best city in the entire world. She loves it here. She'll never leave. You're looking for reasons to love it here." Larkin didn't need to watch Ed to know she was right. Not this time. "And if you get the chance to leave, you'll take it."

"Yeah," Ed said. This time, the tiniest drop of ranch dressing fell off the end of his lettuce leaf, hitting the table before the fork hit his mouth. Larkin waited for him to chew, swallow, and wipe the spot with his napkin. "If something else comes up, I'll probably take it. But I submitted my tenure file to Howell this week, and if they want to keep me on, I'll probably stay."

Something about those two statements didn't make sense. Larkin tried to remember what Anni had said about logical fallacies. "So you're going to continue applying for other jobs?"

"Academics always apply for jobs," Ed said. "It's part of the game."

"Are you applying for other jobs now?"

Ed tried to spear a cherry tomato with his fork; a spray of juice spurted out, and he set his silverware down. "Yeah," he said. "Of course I am."

"Why didn't you tell me?"

"Why would we want to talk about it?"

"I don't know," Larkin said. She stirred at the soggy Os in her cereal bowl. She had barely eaten any of it, and now it was inedible. "Because it's your life? Because it's something you care about? Because you and I both know how the academic job market works? That's another thing we have in common."

"I know," Ed said. "That's why I didn't want to tell you." He looked away—past Larkin, and towards the discussion they'd never really had. "I didn't want to make you feel bad."

Larkin felt terrible. Not because Ed had been trying to protect her—she'd be able to think of that as sweet, or something like that, when she gave herself time to process it—but because she had wanted to be more, to her maybe-sorta boyfriend, than a failed academic. All-but-dissertation, no letters before or after her name, no possibility of a tenure-track job. On the plus side, that meant they'd never have to deal with the two-body problem, assuming they stayed together—Ed could get a faculty job anywhere in the world and they wouldn't have to worry about whether the institution could offer Larkin an equivalent position. On the minus side, it meant that Ed assumed there was still a problem to be dealt with.

"You don't think I wish I were doing the academic job

thing, right?" Larkin asked. "Because I don't—or, wait, do you think I *should* be doing it?"

"I don't know," Ed said. "You're fairly noncompetitive at this point—"

"Thanks—"

"But you're going to need to do *something*, right?"

"I am doing something," Larkin said. "I'm starting a business." The words, when said aloud, sounded uncomfortably familiar. Like *I'm finishing my dissertation.* "And I'm helping people."

"And you're good at that," Ed said. "Which is why—"

"So why did you assume I'd feel bad that you were doing the academic thing and I wasn't?"

"I don't know," Ed said. "It just seemed like something we didn't need to talk about."

These words were also uncomfortably familiar. "I guess that's something else we have in common," Larkin said, knowing she was breaking all of her mother's rules at once —and a few of Claire's. "I've also got something that I didn't want to have to talk to you about."

Ed considered this. Larkin wondered if he already knew what it was. "You know," he said, "you don't have to tell me."

"Well, I probably shouldn't," Larkin said, "because I've been specifically asked *not* to tell you. But before that, I could have said something—and I didn't."

"I know," Ed said. He had to know exactly what she was talking about, which meant that everyone on campus probably knew, which meant that Larkin's mother was less safe than she realized. She should probably tell her mother, as soon as she and Ed were done with lunch—but they hadn't even started the difficult part of their conversation, and Larkin still wasn't sure she'd decided what she wanted to say.

So she made her choice. All four of them, one after the other. It was easier than she expected.

"I think I love you," Larkin said, "because you're smart and kind and you have integrity and you're really interested in what you do and you're really good at making people better." She paused, ready to make a joke about Ed also being extraordinarily good-looking, but she stuck to what needed to be said. "I also think I'm dating you for the wrong reasons. I mean, you can't be someone's girlfriend just because the two of you both like music and art and theater and stuff, and you shouldn't be somebody's girlfriend just because you're looking for someone else who isn't sure they want to stay in Pratincola." She paused, again. Ed was watching her. She waited to see if he would do anything else. Then she continued. "I also think that you think I'm interested in you because you have something that I want. That might be true, a little bit, but it's also a little insulting." She paused, a third time, to see if Ed would take the accusation injuriously. "I mean, I don't want to fight." *Say it.* "I just mean to say that I'm a really interesting person on my own, and so are you, and that doesn't necessarily mean we ought to be together."

Larkin stood up, picking up her tray, trying to keep her hands from shaking. "Because I don't know what we are together, and I think that's something we should know."

Then she walked away, just like her mother had told her to do, sloshing milk over the edge of her cereal bowl and trying not to cry.

———

Larkin had both removed and reapplied her makeup by the time she made it to her mother's office. She was not going to tell her mother that she and Ed had broken up, first because she wasn't quite sure how that could affect Ed's tenure file and second because she wasn't quite sure that they *had*. Could you break up with someone without saying the words? Weren't there other words both of them needed to say first, like *do you want to break up with me* and *no I don't* and *well maybe I don't either*—or maybe *do you want to break up with me* and *yes I do*, either way, but there were sentences that needed to be issued.

Not that they'd needed sentences when they'd started courting. They'd shared enough of an understanding, in what Larkin was still thinking of as *the good old days*, to assume that they would continue to understand each other. Sentience had overruled, turning objection into objectification. The two of them withheld judgment, withheld argument, withheld anything that would not stand cross-examination. They held each other, with or without witnesses. They postponed discovery.

The thing was that nobody else had said a word. Not Ben, who might have noticed Ed's unhappiness; not Anni, who definitely noticed Larkin's. Not Larkin's mother, who had chosen to withdraw from the proceedings due to a preceding conflict of interest. Not even Ed's mother, who had taken just enough of an interest in Larkin to make her comfortable.

The only people who had commented on their potential incompatibility had been people like Bonnie, who said everything that needed to be said with a single physical gesture—and people like Ghoti, who had been careless enough to say it aloud. *You like him because he's hot and he pays attention to you.*

Larkin and Ed went together like sexual tension and contextual release, in other words—and everyone who saw them knew that, and only one person who knew it had said it, and that person was currently sitting on the couch outside of Larkin's mother's office, driving penholes into the smiling faces shining out of a high-gloss Howell college brochure.

"Hello," Ghoti said, without looking up. "I set up the meeting."

"Oh," Larkin said. She had forgotten that both she and her mother had asked Ghoti to get this particular task done. "You probably shouldn't deface that," she said, taking the brochure out of Ghoti's hands. "Pun intended."

"Fine," Ghoti said. "But only because you actually made a pun."

Larkin examined the damage. Ghoti had speared the smiles, not the eyes or the throats or the hearts—and although the majority of the student body had been defanged, a few representatives remained untouched. "Why'd you spare these people?"

"Because they're the only ones who aren't two-faced," Ghoti said.

"That isn't a pun."

"It wasn't intended to be," Ghoti said. They picked up a second copy of the brochure and displayed it to Larkin. "If you were in high school or something, and somebody gave you this brochure, maybe you'd think you were going to a place where everyone smiled all of the time. Maybe you'd think it would be better than high school, where everyone looked at you like you were weird."

"Ghoti," Larkin said. "You didn't enroll in Howell because of this brochure."

"You are correct," Ghoti said. "I did not enroll in Howell because of this brochure."

Larkin flipped through the first three pages. "But you put penholes through all of the people who don't smile all of the time? Or just the people who don't smile when they see you?"

"Same difference," Ghoti said. "Depending on how you look at it."

Larkin continued to look through the brochure. She wanted to see whether Ghoti had punctured her mother's photograph. The brochure was designed to feature the student body, which meant that only a few features belonged to faculty and staff—and although Ghoti had ravaged nearly as many of those visages, Larkin spotted one face that was still fully visible.

"You don't think Ed is two-faced," she said.

"*Dr. Jackson*," Ghoti corrected, "is integrated."

Larkin was about to ask Ghoti whether the *double entendre* was intended—she hoped it wasn't, but with Ghoti, one never knew—when the door opened and a slim, efficient, perfectly put-together teenager stepped out of Larkin's mother's office.

"Aubrey?" the young woman said, ending her question with just enough authority that it didn't need an answer. "The Dean is ready to see you."

Ghoti—and Larkin could suddenly see the years of being *Aubrey*, the toll they must have taken—stood up. "Thanks," they said, before turning to Larkin. "I'll tell your mom you're here, if you want."

"I'll just text her," Larkin said. She took out her phone and sat down in the seat Ghoti had relinquished. The young woman lingered, malignantly, at the door.

"You can make an appointment with me," she said. "Larkin, right?" As before, the question was aimed to intimidate.

"Nah, I got this," Larkin said, keeping her face focused on her phone. "*Janessa*."

It didn't take long for Larkin's mother to text back. It didn't take long for Larkin to find Janessa's photo in the brochure. The student-leader was singularly beautiful and multiracial—which meant that Janessa Martin Lee appeared in either the foreground or the background of nearly every page.

Every single one of her smiles had been stubbed out, which was what Larkin was expecting.

She wasn't expecting to see the picture of Janessa and Ghoti side by side, arms slung over each other's shoulders, the former in a brand-new Howell sweatshirt and the latter with a crumpled Howell sticker pressed into the center of their forehead.

Our students show their spirit in many different ways, the caption read. *How will you Howell?*

Ghoti had pushed the inkpen through both of their faces.

CHAPTER 17

"I really don't think it's anything you need to be worried about," Larkin's mother said, after Ghoti had left her office and Larkin had been allowed in. "First of all, you're not even sure Ed knows about the signs."

"I'm pretty sure," Larkin said. She hadn't told her mother much about her and Ed's fight—she hadn't even told her mother that she and Ed had fought, because she wasn't sure that they actually had, and she definitely hadn't told her mother that she and Ed had broken up, because she wasn't sure they actually hadn't—but she had mentioned what Ed had said about knowing something that Larkin hadn't been telling him.

Which is to say that she had told her mother that Ed probably knew about the signs.

"Second of all," Josephine said, "whoever did this doesn't appear to be escalating." The door that separated her interior office from her exterior one—Larkin wasn't sure if it was called an *anteroom*, although the word came to mind anyway—opened. It was Janessa, informing Dean Day that her next meeting was beginning in ten minutes, and that the meeting's agenda had been sent to her phone along with the previous meeting's agenda and a one-page summary of the minutes.

"Thank you, Janessa," Josephine said. She turned back to Larkin. "Our students are really quite impressive. Janessa is an administrator's dream, and the young person I just met with—"

"Aubrey," Janessa said, calling the name from the doorway before Dean Day could fail to recall it.

"Thank you," Josephine said again, to the door. "I thought their name was Ghoti," she said to Larkin, glancing at a piece of paper on which she had written *Fish*. "Either way, they're extremely intelligent." Then Dean Day picked up her phone, her reading glasses reflecting the documents Janessa had forwarded. "Well," she said—to the agendii, presumably—"this isn't going to be any fun."

"Walk or cart?" Janessa asked, through the door that she had not yet closed.

"Do we have time to walk?" Josephine asked.

"I'd recommend cart," Janessa said. "It's started to snow."

"Thank you," Larkin's mother said for the third time. "I hate the cart," she whispered to Larkin. "It always makes me feel like I'm being carried around on a palanquin."

Janessa brought Dean Day her coat, and the two of them quickly left the administrative building, Larkin following long enough to watch her mother's helpful assistant help her onto a Howell-branded golf cart.

It was, in fact, snowing.

Neither of them offered Larkin a ride.

This left Larkin to walk back to her car, alone, with her hands tucked into her mother's coat pockets. One hand curled around her phone, out of habit; the other held Ghoti's brochure, rolled into a tube and crumpling under her grip. The snowflakes would have fallen onto her nose and eyelashes if she hadn't kept her face down; snow, in Iowa, had fallen off the list of her favorite things after the first snowfall last December. She could still remember the effort it had taken to shovel first the sidewalk and then the driveway, Claire arriving after a day at work to laugh at their lack of progress.

"We are Pacific Northwesterners," Josephine had said. "Snow is not our element."

"You've lived here for eleven years," Claire replied, "and as soon as I finish shoveling you out we're going to build a snowman."

Ed had come by, after Larkin had texted him a photo of the scarved-and-hatted snowpeople her mother and Claire had created. The two of them had added a third snow figure, lumpy and undressed, as Josephine and Claire went inside for coffee and cocoa.

"We're terrible at this," Larkin had said, after their misshapen snowperson had taken its place on the front lawn. The two of them watched, hand in hand, as the head fell off.

"I don't know," Ed had said. "Maybe you could figure out who murdered it."

"Only if you're ready to fill in for its big solo," Larkin had said.

"Hmmm," Ed had said, smiling at her. She had always loved his smile. "Only if you kiss me the way you did before I had to go sing the last one."

That was their last happy day, perhaps. The next day

Larkin asked Ed what she should get his parents for Christmas. "Or maybe it should be from both of us?"

"You don't have to get them anything," Ed said. "I'm going down after finals and I'm going to stay until New Year's."

"All right," Larkin had said. "I guess I won't worry about that."

It had been a lie, even before she said it.

Maybe it would have been different if she'd said something else. Asked Ed to her family's Christmas, as Bonnie had suggested she should have done. Asked Ed *anything*, as Anni had implied she wasn't doing. Asked her mother how to have a difficult conversation and then gone through all four steps, just as she had done at lunch— *decide what you're going to say, stick to what needs to be said, say it,* and *be prepared to walk away.*

No, wait.

There was a step she had missed.

At lunch, and probably at Christmas, and maybe even at Thanksgiving, and who knows how many other important moments.

Larkin pulled her phone out of her pocket and then pulled her fingers out of her gloves. The snow stuck to the screen, making it slick and less haptic—so she tapped out the message as quickly as she could.

Ed I am so sorry

I forgot to listen

Would you like to talk

She turned off her display, put her gloves back on, wiped her phone ineffectually on the outside of her mother's coat, and made it the rest of the way to her car.

As soon as she was inside, she took her phone out again to see if Ed had responded.

He had not—but there were messages from Bonnie, Anni, Ghoti, and Claire.

I did it!

you should see this

I didn't do it

You should see this.

CHAPTER 18

Anni's text had a link attached—but Claire's had an image. Six signs, in a single line, outside Larkin's mother's house.

Dean
Day
Makes
Us
Feel
Unsafe.

Larkin called Claire immediately; she answered on the second ring.

"You saw it?" Claire asked.

"Only the picture you sent. You saw it for real?"

"I'm looking at it right now." Larkin imagined Claire in the living room, standing in front of the picture window—or on the front porch, standing guard.

"I'll be home in a minute," Larkin said, starting the car. "Does Mom know?"

"Not yet," Claire said. "I can't get her to pick up her phone."

Larkin explained, when she returned to the house, that her mother was in some kind of meeting and probably wasn't checking messages; Claire explained that she had found the six messages stuck into the front lawn when she had stopped by the house to check on Pal.

"I still need to take her for her walk," Claire said, "and I want to do it before there's too much snow. Then I need to get back to the station. Can you take care of things for the next few hours?"

"Sure," Larkin said. She wasn't actually sure if she could—she didn't know what she would do, for example, if the people responsible for the signs came back—but she was pretty sure Claire needed reassurance. "I'll call you if anyone approaches the property."

"Great," Claire said, attaching the leash to Pal's collar. "I'll be back for supper. If your mother comes back first, tell her we've got everything under control."

Larkin didn't really think they had everything under control, especially after Claire returned a snow-covered Pal to the house and resumed her duties as an officer of the law, so she set about looking for things to take control of. First, she preheated the oven. Then, she added an egg and a cup of water to a box of brownie mix. Then, she poured the mixture into a well-buttered brownie pan. Lastly, she put the pan into the oven and set her phone's timer to 25 minutes.

She checked the link that Anni had sent, just in case it was relevant to something she could control—but it was an op-ed, in the Cedar Rapids newspaper, about young people and social media. She'd have to ask Anni about that later. She'd text Bonnie back later, too—she could do it now, it would only take a few seconds, but Larkin was uninterested in opening any new conversations.

She was, at that moment, only interested in re-opening the picture Claire had taken.

To look for clues.

Claire had taken the photo right after it had started snowing. Larkin enlarged the image until it pixelated, looking for pixels that were dark enough to pass as footprints. How long had the signs been there before Claire saw them? Were there any tracks, traces, or identifying marks left behind?

Larkin couldn't see anything clearly in the photograph —so she went to the sofa instead, leaning on her knees until her forehead touched the front window. That was when she noticed what had been written on the back side of each sign.

RESIGN.

Six times.

Every letter capitalized.

She wondered if Claire had seen it. She must have—but she hadn't said anything about it, which meant she wasn't worried about Larkin's mother seeing it.

Larkin was. She stared out the window, asking herself if there was any way to take control over this situation. Taking the signs themselves would probably count as destroying evidence, if the situation had in fact escalated to the point at which the signs could be considered *evidence* instead of *garbage*. Taking a picture of the back side of each sign could be useful, since each word had been written slightly differently—one slanted upwards, one slanted downwards, none of the *Ss* were drawn in the same way, either someone had been in a hurry or *multiple somepeople had*—and then Larkin remembered the first sign, and tried to remember where it had ended up. She'd taken it, right? Off the kitchen table? Was it in the guest bedroom somewhere?

That was when her mother got home. Larkin saw the lights first, the car swinging into the driveway, the door slamming closed. The garage door opening. Her mother, covered in snow, tracking it through the kitchen and towards the sofa.

"What are we going to do?" Josephine asked.

"I made brownies," Larkin answered.

"Of course you did," Josephine said. She twitched her nose at Larkin, which Larkin was expecting. Then she put her arms around Larkin's shoulders, which Larkin wasn't. "It's never been like this before," she said. "I've had disagreements with students before, with faculty, with staff—but not like this. Not in my entire career. I don't know what to do."

The oven timer went off. "You're going to eat brownies," Larkin said, giving her mother a hug and then getting up to stick a fork into the center of the brownie pan. There was plenty of brownie goo on the tines—"good, they're ready!"—and she scooped out a center piece for herself and cut an edge piece for her mother. She took her mother's piece out to the sofa—"give me ten minutes, and then I'll make you a coffee with hot chocolate in it"—and carried her own into the guest bedroom.

It was time to find the other signs.

The first one—second one, really—was easy. It was in the closet, stakes still attached, the two pieces of paper still taped over the list of values held within the home. Larkin pulled out her phone to compare handwriting. This person's *RESIGN* matched the *RESIGN* on Sign #6, which meant that the person who created the second sign had also been responsible for writing the word *UNSAFE*.

No, wait.

The sixth sign from the perspective of the sofa would be the first sign from the perspective of the street.

This person had written the word *DEAN*.

Was that important? It could be—but not until Larkin compared this *RESIGN* and its corresponding *ACAB* to the *ACAB* that had been written on the first sign Dean Day received. Where had that one ended up?

"I'm going to go ahead and start the coffee," Larkin's mother called out. "Would you like me to make the full pot?"

"Always," Larkin said.

She'd made coffee that night too, hadn't she? Not that it mattered, she made coffee every night, she made coffee every morning, she made coffee at work, her days were as predictable as the clock on the wall of The Coffee Shop, *time for coffee, time for coffee, time for coffee.*

And the paper—which had been folded into thirds, hadn't it?—had been placed carefully out of the way of the coffee grounds, probably onto the pile of coupons and circulars and receipts that Larkin didn't know why her mother bothered collecting, since coupons and receipts could be clipped and retrieved online, there were apps, but the next day there would have been mail—and the first sign had also come through the mail slot, hadn't it?—and the grocery circulars would have been separated and stacked, and Larkin stood up and practically ran into her mother as the coffee percolated, looking through the flimsy newspaper for the one piece of substantive evidence she had, hoping it hadn't been recycled.

But there it was, folded like a letter with its letters tucked within the folds, and when Larkin took it back to her mother's guest bedroom and reinstated it to its initial state, the initialism revealed itself to be—and she'd noticed this the first time, hadn't she?—a statement shared by multiple writers, one on top of the other.

The individual handwritings yielded to the initial

initials, six subsequent hands tracing variations with varying levels of success. The sequence was easy to follow, once you knew the path each pen had taken. The rest was just as easy to deduce, especially when you could use the photos you'd taken on your phone.

The first layer of letters matched, in expression, the hand that had drawn *DEAN*—the first of the six signs that were still stuck in their yard.

The seventh layer of letters ended with a pinhole—or, as Larkin now understood, a *penhole*.

She texted Ghoti.

You left your signature on the first sign. Why?

There were more important questions to ask, like *why did you stop after the first one* and *who are the other six people* and *are you trying to get my mother to quit her job*, but Larkin knew how to catch a fish.

She also knew she'd have to wait a bit before she could reel Ghoti in—after reading Ghoti's social media, *got called in to work, not my shift but also not my call*—so she used the time to collect the cup of coffee her mother had made, confirm that there were still only six signs in the front yard, ask her mother if they should remove the signs ("let's let Claire decide that one, okay?"), and consider the article Anni had sent her.

Did Smartphones Ruin Your Holiday?

I like to think of myself as a modern man. According to my children, this means I am stuck not only in my ways, but also in the morals and habits of a previous century. They believe that modern life requires them to remain connected at all times to the devices they hold in their hands. I would prefer they connect with the people who love them, especially when we're in the same room together.

Do other parents have this problem? One of my daughters spent the entire Christmas holiday celebrating her smartphone, not her family or the season or, for those of us who are still practicing Christians, the birth of Our Lord. My daughter told us that she needed her phone for work, but I know better. I use my phone for work, just like every other modern man, and it never takes more than a few minutes to make a call or send an email—all of which are handled exclusively between the hours of 9 and 5, Monday through Friday.

No, my daughter was using her phone for the same reason every other young person uses it, these days. The likes! The subscribes! The social media that has changed the meaning of socializing to include every other person in the world—except, of course, dear old Mom and Dad.

I may be a modern man, but I don't want to share my holiday with seven billion other people. My children are used to sharing their lives with everyone they know, as well as plenty of people they've never met—and all without looking up from the glowing screen!

Parents, it's time to take back our family gatherings. Since my daughter chose to spend her Christmas with her apps instead of enjoying her mother's appetizers—which I assure you are not to be missed—I made a choice of my own.

No more phones in my presence.

Otherwise, no Christmas presents—and no birthday presents either!

You have the power to set the same rule. Remember, your children are still children, and you are still their parents. If they do not behave appropriately at family gatherings, you can issue what today's Moms and Dads are calling "a consequence." You can even ask your children to help you enforce that consequence! Adult children are more likely to listen to each other than they are to you, after all—so give one child a reason to get the others to pay attention, and everyone's behavior improves.

Don't believe me? Here's the proof:

The last time my daughters came to visit, we had a very pleasant conversation.

No phones required.

Larkin couldn't figure out why Anni had sent her this piece of drivel—until she scrolled past the article and revealed its author.

David Cooper.

Bonnie's father, assumedly—and Blythe's too.

She texted Bonnie.

What did you do?

Then she went into the kitchen to refill her coffee mug.

"What am I going to do?" Larkin's mother was at the kitchen table, her back to the front window, her laptop open to a series of identical images. "They're everywhere."

She meant, of course, the signs—a single photograph shared across multiple platforms, likes and retweets multiplying with every new view. The total appeared to have passed two thousand, and that was just what Larkin could see over her mother's shoulder.

"You're going to have a difficult conversation," Larkin said.

"Just one?" Larkin's mother switched tabs, keeping tabs on every social network. "I can't imagine."

"Yes," Larkin said, "you can." She knew all about getting people to imagine things. "You told me exactly what to do." There was enough coffee in the pot for one cup; she poured half into her own mug and half into her mother's. Then she tore open a packet of cocoa mix and put half into each brew, being careful to give her mother the majority of the marshmallows.

"Thank you," Josephine said.

Larkin had successfully solved the case of *what her*

mother wanted. Now she needed to solve the problem of *what her mother should do next.* "Tell me who you need to talk to first."

"I don't know," her mother answered. "I should probably start by calling Arnold." Josephine was referring to Arnold Volk, President of Howell College; a gray-haired, steely-eyed son of a soybean farmer who had combined Iowa business sense with Ivy League academic credentials. "I probably should have told him as soon as I saw the first sign."

"Maybe," Larkin said. "But we should focus on your current objective." She almost said *your character's objective,* out of habit. "How would Dean Day like this situation to be resolved?"

"I'd like the students to admit they were wrong and then apologize," Josephine said.

"All right," Larkin said. She was already pretty sure the apology was going to have to go the other way around; even if the students were in fact in the wrong, these stories had a structure as predictable as anything from Ibsen or the Greeks. Her mother was about to confront her *hamartia,* or fatal flaw, and tragedy was likely to follow. "What kind of conversation do you need to have with Howell's president to achieve that outcome?"

"I need to tell him that these students have been harassing me," Josephine said. "And that we should put out a statement telling them to stop."

That was more *hubris* than anything else; Larkin realized that her mother still thought she was in the middle of Act One, not the end of Act Two. "How are you going to get them to stop?"

"I don't know," Larkin's mother said. "I suppose we'd have to have some kind of consequence."

That was the same word Bonnie's father had used.

Larkin's hand was halfway to her phone, ready to see if Bonnie had responded to her text, before she thought better of it. This moment, for better or worse, belonged to her mother.

"What kind of consequence?" Larkin wanted her mother to imagine the worst-case scenario, so she could start thinking of better ones. "Are you going to expel someone for using a slogan associated with a proven record of police violence against Black Americans?"

"Claire hasn't committed any violence against anyone," Josephine said. "They are accusing her of something that she has not done and *will never do*."

"That doesn't matter," Larkin said. "The phrase *all cops are bastards* implies both *some cops are bastards* and *no cops are not bastards*. Even if one of these propositions is false, the other could still be true—and, statistically, it is."

She still wasn't sure she understood this. Her mother, astoundingly, did.

"They're using the Aristotelian argument?"

"Yes," Larkin said.

"That is very impressive," Larkin's mother said. "That means Howell College is doing its job."

"Great," Larkin said. "Now back to your job. What kind of consequence are you going to ask Arnold to lay down?"

"He'd have to let me lay it down," Josephine said, "since I am ultimately responsible for all matters related to Student Affairs."

"So you would be the person punishing the student for accusing you of creating an unsafe environment."

Larkin watched her mother work out the logic of this non-Aristotelian argument. "I probably shouldn't be the person doing that."

"Probably not," Larkin said. "Which means it's time to make another choice."

She watched her mother take her time—and then respond with something that fell between *choice* and *suggestion*. "What if we asked Janessa?"

"Asked her what?"

"What would be best for the student community," Josephine said. "I could fill Arnold in on what has been going on, and then the two of us could ask Janessa to help us develop a path forward."

"What would that path look like?"

"I don't know," Larkin's mother said—but this time, she was smiling. "We could have a seminar where students got to interact with law enforcement professionals. Not just the police, but also lawyers and judges. They could ask questions, and we could share facts and statistics that could help them understand that the Black community in Pratincola is no more at risk of police violence than any other community."

That seemed reasonable enough, as long as the statistics actually proved Josephine's assumptions—and Larkin wasn't at all sure they would—but then Dean Day continued. "No, wait, the first thing we need to do is explain that there is no police violence in Pratincola, I'm pretty sure there isn't, I haven't heard of any, we would know, certainly the students would have rallied in response to anything as terrible as what's been going on in the rest of the country!"

Her smile had expanded into a nervous laugh. Larkin watched her mother's hand clutch at the handle of the coffee mug. "If we can just convince them that no cops in Pratincola are bastards, which can be proved true by numbers, then the logical conclusions will automatically follow! Claire is not a bad person for being a police officer, I am not a bad person for dating her, this was all just an honest misunderstanding based on a sincere drive towards student activism, which we encourage! We want our students to be politically involved! We'll applaud them for a job well done!"

This seemed like the opposite of *a consequence*, and just as bad—but Larkin's mother did not give Larkin the opportunity to intercede. "Political correctness can be incorrect, after all—oh, but nobody says *political correctness* anymore, we'll have to call it something like *Beyond Woke: Applying Facts to Activism.*"

She laughed again. Larkin did not like the sound of her mother's laugh. She wouldn't have called it *laughter*, if she had been directing. She might have called it *fear*.

No—*excitement* and *fear*.

"I'll call Arnold," Josephine continued. "We need to get our plan in place before EOD, if possible."

Larkin tapped her phone to check the time—2:13—and then her messages.

I got my phone to work! That was from Bonnie.

I'm at work. That was from Ghoti.

See you at 4 for class?

I'm on break at 2:15 if you want to talk.

Guided fitness was at the bottom of Larkin's priority list at the moment. Finding Ghoti was at the top, and it would take five minutes to drive over to the campus bookstore. She could be back before her mother had the chance to put any plans into place, assuming Ghoti's break was fifteen minutes long.

"I gotta do a thing," Larkin said. "Will you be okay by yourself until 2:30 or so?"

"Of course," Josephine said, twitching her nose at Larkin. Her smartphone was pressed to her ear, even though you didn't need to do that anymore. "I'm on hold."

"Keep holding," Larkin said, twitching her nose back. "And don't leave the house until I get back."

"Why?" her mother asked, as Larkin zipped up her hand-me-down coat and stuffed her jeans into the sides of her boots.

Larkin thought about invoking the snow—which was now falling at a rate that suggested she would need to drive with both her lights and her windshield wipers on— but she knew her mother had been dealing with Iowa weather for much longer than she had.

So she put an even greater threat in her mother's path.

"Because you don't want anyone to take your picture and post it online."

CHAPTER 19

Larkin's car slid softly towards the first four-way stop sign. It skidded towards the second. She made it to the campus bookstore in seven minutes, leaving her roughly the same amount of time to find Ghoti and have what would probably be a difficult conversation.

Luckily, Ghoti was easy to locate—the same table, the same hunch.

That gave them six minutes.

"Hello," Larkin said. "I came to talk."

"You drove over here?" Ghoti turned their phone face-down and turned their face towards Larkin. "You know that supercomputer in your pocket both makes and receives calls."

Larkin had once again forgotten that her smartphone was also a *phone*. "I wanted to talk," she said. "In person."

"Just like a real detective," Ghoti said. "Hercule Poirot would have done the same." They paused. "Miss Marple might have just sent a card."

Five minutes.

"So you figured out that I figured out it was you," Larkin said.

"I thought you figured out it was me the first time we talked," Ghoti said. "You were standing, like, *right over there*, and you told me that your mom's girlfriend couldn't be a bastard because she was conceived within the holy bonds of wedlock." They smiled. "That was a *very* Poirot thing to do. Miss Marple wouldn't even have said the word *bastard*."

"And then you said you'd stop doing the signs," Larkin said.

"I did," Ghoti said, "and I did you one better. I got everyone else to stop doing the signs, too."

"No, you didn't."

"Yes," Ghoti said, "I did."

Four minutes.

"No, wait, you're right," Ghoti said. "I didn't."

Larkin didn't have any idea what Ghoti was talking about—and then she did. "Many people made the first sign," she said. "Only one person made the second."

"You're counting them all as one sign?"

"Well," Larkin said, "I guess it had two sides."

Then she realized that Ghoti had no idea what she was talking about. "There was a second sign," she explained. "Before the six signs that went up this afternoon. It just had one person's writing on it, not, like, seven people writing on top of each other."

"That was my idea," Ghoti said. "From *Murder on the Orient Express*."

Larkin knew she should have some idea of what Ghoti was talking about, but she hadn't had enough extra cash to see the movie when it came out—and she'd never been all that interested in mystery novels. She'd ask Claire about it, later.

"It was way better than that Burma Shave thing they did in your mom's front yard," Ghoti continued. "But that was the one that went viral."

Now Larkin had no idea what Ghoti was talking about, except for the part where the signs were all over social media.

"My ideas never go viral," Ghoti said. "I should have known."

Three minutes.

"Why'd you leave a penhole in the first sign?" Larkin asked Ghoti.

"Why do you think?"

Larkin did not want to think—but the first thing she thought of was *so I would know it was you*, and then she thought *no, Ghoti didn't even know me when they made the first sign*, and so she said "So somebody would know you'd done it."

"Wrong," Ghoti said.

"But the penhole is your signature."

"Wrong again."

All right, Larkin thought, *then what is it?* At this point, she'd seen Ghoti punch holes in a bag of gummy worms and a brochure. How were those connected to the signs? The bag of gummy worms probably didn't count, except for the part where Ghoti had used an inkpen instead of fingers or scissors or teeth. *The smiles*—and Larkin said "Because you were being two-faced."

Two minutes.

"You didn't want to do it," Larkin said. "But you also wanted to do it."

Why?

"Because you wanted—"

What did Ghoti want?

"Friends."

Ghoti nodded.

"But it didn't work." Larkin had never seen Ghoti interact with another student—except, of course, the brief interaction with Janessa outside of the Dean's office. "You thought if you did this thing then people would smile at you when they passed you on the quad, or whatever. They didn't."

Ghoti shrugged.

"But the other students who made the signs must have liked you," Larkin said. "I mean, you were able to convince them to stop. That takes leadership."

"Leadership isn't the same thing as friendship," Ghoti said, "and being right isn't the same thing as being liked." They checked the time on their phone—one minute, probably—and stood up. "Anyway, it doesn't matter. She found more people to help her. She'll always find people to help her. People like her are, like, *viral humans*."

"Who?"

"*Whom*."

"Ghoti, we don't have time for this, Blythe's going to be here any minute asking where you are—"

"Not today," Ghoti said, putting their employee lanyard back on. "I'm covering for Blythe. She called out, and the big boss called me." They winked at Larkin—or maybe it was just a blink, it was hard to tell when you could only ever see one of Ghoti's eyes at a time. "Which means I do pick up my phone."

"Fine," Larkin said. "Next time I'll use my pocket supercomputer for its original purpose. Are you going to tell me *whom* it is?"

"Well," Ghoti said, "it's obviously the person who made the second sign. I know that, and I haven't even seen it."

"It looked just like the first sign," Larkin said, "except

it said *ACAB* on one side and *RESIGN* on the other." She followed Ghoti into the bowels of the Howell bookstore. "And it only had one person's handwriting."

"And it didn't work," Ghoti said, three steps ahead of Larkin.

"Why?"

"Because your mother is still Dean of Howell College," Ghoti said. "At least for now."

That was when the power went out.

CHAPTER 20

There were no windows in the Howell College bookstore—but there were plenty of phones. Some people activated Flashlight Mode right away; others, including Larkin, were distracted by their newest texts and messages.

Happy to talk, Ed had sent. *Maybe after Bonnie's class?*

Going to Howell to meet with the Prez, Larkin's mother had sent. *Will avoid the paparazzi.*

did you read the article? Anni had sent.

Larkin ignored Anni. She sent a quick *yes* to Ed, then added *thanks*, then added a heart emoji. Even if they ended up breaking up, she could still love him for being happy to talk with her after she'd failed to listen.

Her mother had also failed to listen—and so Larkin asked Ghoti, one more time, "Are you going to tell me who made the signs?"

"Snitches get stitches," Ghoti said. "If you can't figure it out on your own, you probably shouldn't be a detective."

"Do you think my mother's job is a joke?"

"I think the entire concept of higher education is a joke," Ghoti said. "You should have been able to figure that one out on your own, too."

Larkin saw Ghoti's single visible eye turn away from her. "And now I gotta go figure out if I'm going to get paid for working in the dark." She heard, but did not see, Ghoti sigh. "At least Blythe's birthday party or whatever got ruined."

"Wait, what?"

Larkin waited for Ghoti to tell her what else she had failed to figure out on her own.

"Blythe called out," Ghoti called out, "because it was her birthday."

———

Larkin began plowing her way through ankle-high snowdrifts, leaving a trail of boot prints behind her. This would have been an excellent time to have had access to her mother's palanquin, although Larkin didn't really know how well golf carts handled in snow. Janessa would, of course. Janessa was another one of those people who knew everything. Larkin seemed to know a lot of those kinds of people, and for some reason they all seemed to like her. One of these days she'd figure out why.

Today she had to figure out who had drawn the second sign.

She also had to figure out what she was going to say to Ed, after Bonnie's class, before she started listening.

She also had to figure out—and it didn't feel like a thing she'd had to figure out until it *did*—why Bonnie was holding her class while Blythe was missing work.

Obviously it was because Bonnie liked working.

And Bonnie had gotten her phone to work.

And if there was some kind of birthday party that Blythe had called out for, Bonnie would still have plenty of time to participate. Nobody threw a party for twin twentysomethings at 2 p.m. on a Monday, after all.

Was Blythe planning the party?

This was the least important question on Larkin's mind, which was probably why her mind was so eager to answer it. Blythe had to have called off early to do *something*, unless she just wanted an excuse to skip work, which was completely reasonable—though not completely responsible. Bonnie was apparently the good twin, and Blythe was the bad one. It made sense, given the state of their respective parental gifts; vehicles for their inner selves, as cars so often were.

Except Blythe had said that she was the good twin.

Which made Bonnie the bad one.

Which also made sense—if two conflicting ideas could make sense at the same time—given that their dad had written that entire op-ed about Bonnie. Right? It was too cold and too wet for Larkin to want to check the article—but hadn't David Cooper written about a *daughter* who had ruined the family holiday with her smartphone? She hadn't been present, he was going to withhold presents, everyone in Pratincola was obsessed with puns, you couldn't talk to an Eastern Iowan without working in wordplay—

Larkin stopped walking. A chunk of snow slid into the inside of her boot.

Bonnie had just gotten her phone to work.

Bonnie and Blythe got identical, expensive presents.

Bonnie and Blythe's father had threatened to withhold those presents if his children didn't behave at family gatherings.

Bonnie and Blythe's father got his children to help him enforce his rules.

Blythe had gotten out of work to prevent Bonnie from using her phone.

Larkin's feet were getting very wet—and very cold. She peeled off her mother's gloves and pulled out her phone, trying to decide what to text Bonnie. *Watch out* seemed a little premature, and *your sister wants to make sure you get your birthday presents, so don't spend your entire party on your phone* seemed a little immature.

She went with *can we talk before class?*

This gave her a little over an hour to find her mother, tell her mother—wait, what was she supposed to tell her? The snow was making it difficult for Larkin to think clearly.

It was also making it difficult for her to see more than a few inches in front of her.

So she turned on her phone's flashlight and began to inch her way forward, wobbling every few steps as her boots failed to secure themselves against the sidewalk. She was supposed to tell her mother that there had been a coordinated student effort to get Dean Day to resign. That there *was* a coordinated student effort—Larkin flailed, waved her arms, landed on her butt—and that Ghoti had successfully convinced the first group of students that it wasn't worth the effort, but a second group of students had emerged.

Under the same student-leader, to borrow her mother's phrase.

Larkin raised herself to a squatting position. Her feet were completely soaked. Her phone was securely in her hand, but the flashlight had temporarily given way to a low battery notification—and before Larkin could resume her illumination, she had to peel off her gloves and swipe the warning off the screen.

Which didn't work with wet hands.

Then she saw another light—twin lights, actually. Brighter than her flashlight, and rapidly approaching.

It was the Howell-branded golf cart.

Larkin stood up and waved her arms. "Hello," she called out, "don't hit me!"

The golf cart stopped. "I'm not going to hit you," Janessa said—because of course it was Janessa, how lucky it was for Larkin to have encountered Janessa right then, theater people always made jokes about economy of character but this was *fate*, the perfect person to help her mother was right here *and she had a golf cart*—and Larkin stumbled forward until she had gripped the side of the cart with both hands.

The top half of Janessa's face was obscured by faux fur; her lipstick, underneath the fringe of mink or rabbit or whatever it wasn't, was perfect. "Oh," she said, smiling—Janesssa had to be smiling, even though Larkin couldn't see her eyes to make sure—"it's you."

"Yes," Larkin said. "I need your help—it's for my mom, it's a dean thing, it's a very important dean thing, and I know you're probably doing something administrative with that golf cart but maybe you could use it to help me get to the President's Office?"

"Why?"

"Because there are these students—" Larkin stopped, suddenly unsure of whether she should trust Janessa. Ghoti hadn't trusted Janessa. Ghoti had put a penhole through the one part of Janessa's face that was currently visible, after learning about the part that Janessa kept hidden. Larkin should have understood this. She should have understood everything.

"These students?" Janessa started the golf cart again. "You mean the ones with the signs?"

"Yes," Larkin said. "Are you going to give me a ride?" Janessa didn't have to be trustworthy, as long as she saw the worth of helping Larkin help her mother save her job. The two faces went both ways, after all.

"What are you going to do?" Janessa asked. "Try and stop them?"

"No," Larkin said. "That's what my mom's trying to do. I'm trying to stop my mother from resigning."

She put one snow-slick, booted foot on the edge of the golf cart, ready to swing herself up into the passenger seat. Janessa swerved, jerking Larkin off the cart and into the snow. Larkin felt her tailbone hit cement, the shock cascading up her spine even with six inches of snow and twelve inches of hand-me-down puffy coat as a buffer. Her right wrist hit next, colliding with what must have been some kind of decorative border rock before all borders had been decorated and then obscured by snow. Larkin withdrew her arm; the impact had drawn blood.

"Hey!" she said. "What was that about?"

"Figure it out," Janessa said—just like Ghoti had. "I'm late for a meeting with the president and the soon-to-be-former dean."

She glanced back at Larkin as the golf cart glided over the snow-covered sidewalk—and Larkin saw Janessa's face slip out of its hood.

Her eyes were not smiling.

They were gleaming with delight—and as the lights of the golf cart disappeared into the curtain of still-falling snow, Larkin realized that she had absolutely no idea what to do next.

CHAPTER 21

Larkin's phone buzzed. Then it issued a long, steady beep, which it wasn't supposed to do— none of her settings were set that way—and when she fumbled for it and pulled it out of the falling snow and unzipped her mother's coat to wipe the screen against the lining, she saw a message from the National Weather Service. *Winter Storm Warning*, as if Larkin didn't already know it was storming. As if anybody in Pratincola needed to be warned. *Take shelter*, the message continued, before taking up just enough of Larkin's remaining battery for her to hesitate before turning on the flashlight.

She had to warn her mother, after all.

Not about the storm. She was pretty sure her mother already knew about that.

About Janessa.

She hadn't guessed it in time—she'd have to ask Ghoti why they didn't just *tell her*, later—but she still had time to make it to the administrative office building.

First, a text: *Don't let Janessa into the meeting.*

Then, a first step—wobbly, wet, her tailbone aching, her wrist pulsing, her heartbeat racing.

A response: *I'm already in the meeting.*

A second step—slippery, slick, her socks soaked, her fingers freezing, the blood from her wrist uncomfortably warming the space between palm and glove.

A second response: *And I have your mother's phone.*

"How does she—" Larkin said, but then she saw it, her mind creating how it might have gone, the National Weather Service issuing its warning, the sirens going off, her mother handing the phone to Janessa because she didn't know how to make it stop. Or, maybe, her mother turning off the siren herself and leaving the phone face-up on the table as she talked to President Vogt about what needed to be done about the signs. Janessa, entering the room and seeing the incoming text. Intercepting.

Except—Larkin could call her mother, both of them had set up their phones so calls from the other always went through, Josephine would be sure to pick up, this was a solvable problem—and yet when Larkin pulled her right hand out of its glove, noting the blood, ignoring the blood, hoping she was making the right call, she found herself unable to get through.

The phone rang, of course. It rang as if it had been turned to silent—which is what Janessa must have done after seeing Larkin's message. Ghoti would be impressed at everything Larkin was guessing correctly, now that it was too late to have guessed right.

What was left? To walk to the office, assumedly. To knock on the door. To demand to be let in, so that she could tell everyone involved—but Janessa would tell them herself, probably. She'd be proud of her work on the signs. She'd be able to put Dean Day's resignation on her resume.

Resigned, Larkin resumed. Three steps. Four. Her phone flashed a low battery notification. She had to take her hand out of her glove again to wipe it away. Her fingers left pink stains on the screen. What were you supposed to do with injured body parts? RICE, right? Rest, ice, something that started with C, and elevation? Larkin already had the ice part, and the elevation. She'd do the rest later.

Five. This was going nowhere fast, although her mother would forgive the cliché if she made it to the administrative office in time. Six. Maybe she could find another golf cart. Seven. Maybe she could get someone else to help her. Eight. No, not *him*. Nine. She wasn't sure he was still on campus. Ten. She wasn't sure she wanted to be the kind of girlfriend who needed to be rescued. Eleven. She wasn't even sure she was still his girlfriend. Twelve—and Larkin fell, smacking her non-dominant wrist against the pavement and dropping her phone a second time.

"Forks!" Larkin shouted, falling back on Anni's preferred phrases and sending them into the storm. "Focaccia bread! Fun-sized candy bars!" Unfortunately, only the full-sized words would do. "Fuuuuuu—"

The response came, through the snow—

"Don't you mean *blow, winds, and crack your cheeks?*"

It was Ed. His arms were around hers, his gloved fingers were examining her bruised and bleeding wrists, he was lifting her up and helping her towards what turned out to be his car.

"We're here," he said, opening the passenger door and settling Larkin inside.

"You quoted *Lear* to me," Larkin said.

"Everyone wants to play Lear someday," Ed said. "Today, I'm playing Kent."

"No," Larkin said, "Superman." She almost kissed him. She almost cried. "And I'm playing the fool."

"Why?" Ed asked. "Because of what happened at lunch? We can talk about that if you want. I've been wanting to have that conversation for a while." He started the car. "We should probably have it somewhere warm, though. Do you want to go back to my apartment?"

"Yes," Larkin said, "but we have two places we need to go first." She sat up, buckled her seatbelt, and checked the clock on Ed's dashboard. Her own phone had been thrown into a snowdrift the second time she fell; there wasn't enough time to retrieve it, not when her mother was about to be usurped by a student-leader and her client was about to be disinherited—no, wait, if it was really about birthday presents, it would be *inherited*—by an evil twin.

She explained all of this to Ed, as well as she could, in the minutes between 2:43 and 2:45.

"All right," he said, "I'll give you a ride to the administrative office, and then we'll go to the fitness center." He flicked on his brights, cranked up his wipers, and slowly backed the car out of its parking space. "I'd ask you if you had a plan, but I know you too well."

"Does that mean you know I have a plan, or you know I don't have a plan?" Larkin asked. "Because I could see it going either way."

"Yes," Ed said, "and either way, I'm rooting for you."

If Larkin didn't have two mysteries to solve—or, more accurately, two crimes to prevent—in just under an hour, she would have asked Ed whether he was also rooting for the two of them, as a couple. But there would be time for that afterwards. Time for all the words. Right now Ed was driving, tooting his horn at every intersection, and pulling carefully into the administrative office parking lot—and Larkin was thinking.

And then she was getting out of the car.

"You understand why I'm going to sit this one out, right?" Ed kept both his car and his wipers running.

"Of course," Larkin said. Her boots sank into snow deep enough that it would have soaked her socks if they weren't already waterlogged. "You understand that's why I didn't tell you about any of this earlier, right?"

"Of course," Ed said. "And you understand that I knew the whole time, right?"

"Yeah," Larkin said, "but I can't figure out how you knew. We kept those first few signs a secret."

"You and your mother may have," Ed said, "but Ghoti didn't."

"Wait, *what*?"

"Ghoti told me as soon as they were asked to make the first sign," Ed said. "They asked if I would think more of them or less of them for participating. I said it only mattered what they thought of themselves."

"Wow," Larkin said. "I can see why Ghoti likes you. You're amazing."

"What I am is *freezing*," Ed said. "Now *go*. You have one hour and two jobs to save."

CHAPTER 22

Larkin's first instinct, once she had climbed the snow-covered steps and passed under awning and doorway, was to unzip her boots and strip off her socks. She rubbed her wet feet against the flat academic carpet, thinking of Ghoti and the water fountain and her earlier question about how often the Howell carpets got cleaned. That was something for someone like Anni to be concerned about, though—and she owed Anni a text, she shouldn't forget that—and could wait until after she had finished her current job.

Which was, of course, *helping her mother save hers.*

Just as soon as she got her feet warm.

Her sodden gloves deposited next to her socks, Larkin made a quick stop at the washroom to grab a wad of paper towels. Halfway down the hall she wondered if she should have washed the scrape on her wrist with soap before attempting to stanch it; another question for Anni. Or her mother, really. Mothers were the best people for knowing those kinds of things.

But Larkin's mother hadn't known that Janessa wasn't

the best person to hire as her assistant—but maybe she had been, when she started her work-study job. Janessa's face could have flipped, later, proving Dean Day's judgment right before it was wrong.

Now Larkin stood before the double doors that led to the President's Office, wondering which hand would be least likely to sully the gold-plated handle. Both were still wet; the blood seeping from her wrist had made its way onto all ten of her fingertips.

Well, it wasn't like they wouldn't know it was her, so she didn't need to worry about leaving prints—and Larkin pressed a pink palm against the handle and pushed.

The door was locked.

She curled her palm into a fist, ready to knock—or bang, if necessary—and then she heard voices.

PRESIDENT VOLK: This would have to go through our Board of Directors.

DEAN DAY: They'd never approve it.

PRESIDENT VOLK: They might, actually.

JANESSA: I'm sure they'd approve of anything that would benefit admissions. Think of the press Howell would receive. You'd be venerated, really. More importantly, you'd go viral.

DEAN DAY: You mean you'd go viral.

JANESSA: We've already established that I'm doing this in service of Howell College.

Larkin imagined the scene—her mother, seated, halfway down the long wooden table where the Board would eventually meet. President Volk, pacing clockwise around the table; Janessa, walking confidently in the other direction. Every time their paths met, they would pass each other a look—animosity turning into curiosity, adversary into admiration.

DEAN DAY: But you're not qualified to serve. It takes years—

JANESSA: Why should it take years? Who better to act as Dean of Student Affairs than someone who has immediate, relevant experience *as a student*?

PRESIDENT VOLK: She has a point.

DEAN DAY: She's *making* a point. That doesn't make it true.

Larkin heard only one set of footsteps; she reset the stage. Janessa seated calmly at the head of the table; her mother, less calmly, at the foot. The president could keep pacing, not in circles this time, but in an arc between the two women. Trying to find common ground.

JANESSA: You need someone on your administrative team who can truly advocate for the needs of the students.

DEAN DAY: Do you think I don't advocate for your needs? The fact that you were employed in my office—

JANESSA: Not technically employed. Invited to work for free.

DEAN DAY: Invited to gain valuable experience that can help you in your future career!

JANESSA: And why can't I use this valuable experience to generate value *right now*?

DEAN DAY: For Howell or for yourself?

JANESSA: Ideally, both. This is a revenue-generating idea, and because of that we can negotiate an appropriate compensation.

PRESIDENT VOLK: You're still a student.

JANESSA: I'll graduate this spring. Dean Day can finish out the semester as she prepares for the next phase of *her* future career. We could formalize the transition at the graduation ceremony, maybe—or if you'd rather have two separate news events, announce at graduation and formalize in the fall.

A pause. Larkin considered knocking. She waited.

DEAN DAY: Arnold, you can't seriously be considering this.

PRESIDENT VOLK: It would have to go through the Board.

DEAN DAY: I would have to resign!

Another pause.

PRESIDENT VOLK: You could be voted out.

DEAN DAY: I have tenure.

PRESIDENT VOLK: Yes. We could make a place for you on the faculty, if you preferred.

DEAN DAY: Preferred to *what*?

The electricity flickered. Larkin wondered if the room on the other side of the door was lit by flashlight, candlelight, or nothing more than the emergency bulbs that had generated enough illumination for her to make it safely down the hallway.

JANESSA: That could make the story even more saleable—maybe. Dean recommends student-leader before retiring to her former position in the poetry department.

DEAN DAY: Howell doesn't have a poetry department. It has an English department, which you would know if you had *any institutional knowledge whatsoever*.

The power went back on.

PRESIDENT VOLK: And Josephine never had a position in the English department. She was hired directly as dean, seven years ago.

DEAN DAY: I'm actually finishing my eleventh year at Howell.

PRESIDENT VOLK: Has it been that long?

The power went off again.

JANESSA: You know, most modern universities are reconsidering the tenure system. It makes these kinds of transitions much more difficult. Even among the faculty—

when Dean Day joined Howell, for example, social media didn't even exist. I'd find it difficult, as a student, to take a poetry class from a person who was unaware of "The Tiger."

Larkin waited for her mother to walk into the trap.

DEAN DAY: You cannot mean the poem by William Blake.

JANESSA: I mean the poem written by a six-year-old in an urban nonprofit literacy center. I could recite it, if you like. Nearly every student at Howell could.

Larkin didn't believe that, but it didn't matter—she could tell, by the pause in President Volk's pacing, that he did.

JANESSA: This is the kind of institutional knowledge Howell needs. I'm sure I'll pick up the rest fairly quickly. Sorry about the poetry department error, Dr. Day. Maybe we should create one.

DEAN DAY: There isn't enough money in the budget to create a new department. There wouldn't even be enough money to keep me on as faculty.

JANESSA: Then it looks like the solution is obvious. We all need to do what is best for Howell.

President Volk began pacing again.

DEAN DAY: Is this really because of my relationship with Claire Novak?

JANESSA: Of course not, although it was never a good look for you—or the college. You would have known that, if you were aware of the world today's students are trying to create. I simply took that awareness and used it as an opportunity to demonstrate my capacity for leadership. I recruited two unique groups of student-activists to partici-pate in a project that has in fact proved effective.

DEAN DAY: You mean you got two groups of students to stick unsigned signs into my front lawn.

PRESIDENT VOLK: She has a point.

Larkin couldn't tell whether the president was referring to Janessa, or to her mother—but it didn't matter. She suddenly understood what she could do to help, as long as she could convince one unique student to help her.

That was when Larkin—barefooted, bloody-fingered—turned and ran as fast as she could, down the hallway, out the door, scooping up her boots, socks, and gloves along the way. She was able to step, barefoot, into each of her previous bootprints; Ed saw her coming and stripped off his wool scarf even before she got into the car.

"Thank you," Larkin said, wiping and warming her feet.

"What happened? Are you still bleeding?"

"It's all right," Larkin said, holding up her right wrist. "Pun intended."

She watched Ed smile. She didn't know how many more of those smiles she'd get to see after they had their relationship-defining discussion, but this one was enough.

"Do you need me to take you home?" Ed asked. "Or are we still moving forward with the plan?"

"Plan, plan, *plan!*" Larkin said. She watched Ed watch *her* smile, and then watched the same question pass through his mind—*how many more times will I get to see this?*

They'd answer that question later. "I need to be in and out of the campus bookstore in ten minutes," Larkin continued, putting her bare feet directly into her boots and zipping them up. "And then we gotta go to guided fitness."

CHAPTER 23

The power was back on, in full, by the time Ed pulled into the parking lot—which meant that Larkin could use the campus streetlights to avoid the deepest drifts of snow. Her feet were cold, but not damp, and anyway it didn't matter, she could make it through the next forty minutes and then she could sit in the Pratincola Fitness Complex sauna for as long as she wanted to.

She and Ed could have their conversation in the sauna, if they wanted to.

That would be interesting—but she couldn't think about that right now, she still had two jobs to save, *come on, Larkin, get those slippery feet into the bookstore and find that Ghoti*, and there they were, tidying an aisle of Howell-branded throw blankets.

"Do you want to stop being two-faced?" Larkin asked.

"Have you switched from private investigation to public service announcement?"

"Yes," Larkin said. "I am announcing the opportunity for you to serve in public."

Ghoti eyed Larkin. They ran their hands over a bit of fleece, picking out a piece of lint. "I'm only supposed to talk to customers."

"Fine," Larkin said. "I'm buying that blanket."

"It costs a hundred and thirty dollars," Ghoti said.

"*Fine*," Larkin said. "Now listen. Janessa is in the President's Office right now staging a coup. There's something you can do to help, but I can't tell you what it is because it can't look like it was my idea. You have to figure it out on your own."

"What if I don't care what happens to your mother?"

"What if my mother cares what happens to you?" Larkin knew what Ghoti wanted, and she knew how to offer it. "She said you were one of the smartest students she'd ever met. Don't you want someone like her in charge? Do you really want Howell to be run by someone like Janessa?"

"It doesn't matter what I want," Ghoti said.

"Yes, it does," Larkin said. "What you want matters, and what you do matters, and if you don't like what you're doing you can do something else and see if it gets you closer to what you want."

"That is literally Theater 101."

"Good, because I used to teach Theater 101."

"Is that why Dr. Jackson likes you?"

"I don't know," Larkin said, "but we are literally going to ask each other this very question in about two hours." She wondered if Ed would like her less for telling Ghoti their personal business. She decided it only mattered whether or not she liked herself—and right now, she was pretty good with being Larkin Day. "That's what adults do, by the way. We create relationships that have never existed before, that don't have to follow the rules of liking someone because they're hot or wanting to be someone's friend because they're popular, all that matters is that we agree on what exists between us, and that gives us as many possibilities as a newly-shuffled deck of cards."

She was kind of being Anni Morgan there, a little—and she still owed Anni a text, although she didn't know how she was going to text Anni if her phone was lost in the snow somewhere between the bookstore and the administrative office—and then Ghoti said "Fifty-two factorial."

"What?"

"The number of possibilities." Ghoti brushed their hair out of their eye and smiled at Larkin. "What do you want me to do?"

"I want you to figure it out on your own. I can't be involved."

"Can I buy a vowel?"

"It costs a hundred and thirty dollars," Larkin said.

She watched Ghoti register that neither of them would be carrying that blanket to the Howell-branded cash register. "*Fine*," Ghoti said.

Larkin took a deep breath. "Oh captain, my captain!" she said, hoping Ghoti would get both the reference and the message.

They did.

"I can't," Ghoti said. "There's too much snow."

"Then I will quote another poet," Larkin said. "*Welcome to college, here's your right-click.*"

Ghoti got it, again, and took out their phone.

———

As soon as Larkin was back in Ed's car, she said "You need to text Anni."

"Why?" Ed was retracing his wheeltrails out of the parking lot, just carefully enough that Larkin knew he wanted to hurry. The clock on the dashboard read 3:31—not a lot of time to get to the fitness center and get in touch with Bonnie.

"Because she texted me, and—" Larkin decided she didn't have time to explain the whole thing. "Because my phone got lost in the snow when Janessa threw me out of the golf cart."

"So you want me to text," Ed said. "While I'm driving."

"Everybody does it!" Larkin said. "You can do it at a stop sign."

"Absolutely not," Ed said. "I will spare you the safety lecture, skip the statistics on how many young Black men are pulled over for minor traffic violations—yes, even in Pratincola—and simply remind you that *my entire car is a phone.*"

They pulled, carefully, towards a four-way stop. "Call Anni Morgan," Ed said aloud.

"She won't pick up," Larkin said—but she did.

"Hello, Ed!" Anni's voice, capable and cheerful, filled the car. "How are you doing?"

"Very well," Ed said, "although I have an injured unlicensed private detective in my car who very much wants to talk to you."

"Larkin! What happened? Are you all right?"

"Yes," Larkin said. Her right wrist was mostly not-bleeding. "I lost my phone in a fight and Ed rescued me. I'll tell you everything later, *if you ask.*"

Anni laughed. Larkin relaxed, despite her bruises and contusions. They were good—they had probably always been good, even while Anni was drafting and saving and sending her letter. That was all that mattered.

"So how can I help you now?" Anni asked, efficient and ebullient.

"You can help me figure out if today is Blythe and Bonnie Cooper's birthday."

"That's easy." That was Elliott. Of course Elliott would be with Anni—and of course Anni would have put Ed and Larkin on speaker. "Blythe and Bonnie Cooper are turning 23 today. Born February 6."

"Was that a Sunday?" Larkin asked, remembering something her mother had said when this all started.

"Yes, actually," Elliott said. "You're not one of those people who can figure out calendar days in their head, right?"

"It's a poem," Larkin and Ed said at the same time. "The child born on the Sabbath Day," Ed began; Larkin finished, "is blithe and bonny and something and gay."

"Good and gay, right?" Ed asked.

"We'll figure it out later," Larkin said. They'd figure everything out later, and they'd do it together. Larkin and Ed, even if they stopped being Larkin-and-Ed, were also good—and that was also all that mattered.

"Next question," Larkin said. "Is Bonnie holding her class this afternoon?"

"Yes," Elliott said. "The Pratincola Fitness Complex remains open."

"Even though the National Weather Service advised us to seek shelter?"

"We don't worry too much about National Weather Service warnings in Pratincola," Anni said. "If we stopped the town every time we got one, we'd never get anything done."

"And the fitness center is serving as a temporary warming shelter for people in need," Elliott explained. "They've got a box of donated coats and plenty of free hot cocoa."

"And classes are running as usual?"

"Any instructors who want to teach may proceed as scheduled," Elliott confirmed.

"Bonnie will want to teach," Larkin said. "Which means we can't let her class proceed as scheduled." She took a deep breath, making sure she really wanted to say what she thought she needed to say next. "Elliott, I need you to lock Bonnie out of her fitness instructor dashboard."

"Why?"

"Can you do it?"

She listened, over Ed's speaker, to the sounds of Elliott thinking. "Yes," he said. "Her account should still be active on my old laptop. I can change the password from there."

"Great," Larkin said. "Do it."

"Why?" Elliott asked again. "Locking Bonnie out of her account is easy enough, but once she gets the notification that her password has been updated, she can report an unauthorized password change and get her account back."

"Of course she can," Larkin said, as if she had known that all along. "We're not trying to, like, *re-murder* her. We're just trying to stall her. We're trying to stop her class from happening."

"Why?" This time it was Anni who asked.

"So we have a chance to talk to her about Blythe, and their birthday, and whether they're expecting some big present from their dad that they're not going to get if Bonnie uses her phone during the party."

"They are," Anni said. "I heard Bonnie talking about it after class, right after New Year's. They're each getting five grand. She doesn't want it."

"How can you not want five thousand dollars?" If Larkin had $5,000 she would pay off her credit card debt and buy a new coat and new boots and new socks and new gloves and a new scarf for Ed, since she had gotten snowmelt and wrist blood all over the one he just loaned her.

"She made it her New Year's Resolution to become financially independent from her parents."

"And Blythe," Larkin deduced, "did not."

She checked Ed's clock. "Which means we don't know what Blythe's going to do, but we do know that she called out of work to do it. There's something afoot, I swear—"

"*Foot* is an excellent fake swear word," Anni said, "I'm adding it to my list—"

"And we won't be able to figure it out unless we stop that class from happening." Larkin took another deep breath and redelivered her line. "Elliott, kill Bonnie's access to her dashboard."

"You're lucky I'm a rogue," Elliott said, "and you're even luckier that I'm Chaotic Neutral."

The sound of typing; the sound of Ed's tires skidding slightly in the snow.

"Done," Elliott said. "I hope that was the best use of our move."

———

They arrived at the fitness center complex at 3:52. The two of them ran inside, hand in hand—Larkin suspected Ed was holding her hand just to keep hers warm, since she had long abandoned her gloves—and raced past cups of cocoa and boxes of coats. Larkin wanted one of those cups of cocoa. She also wanted one of those coats. But she had everything she needed, at least for now— and she had to stop Blythe from going after what she wanted.

Or maybe she had to stop Bonnie from going after what Blythe didn't want.

She wasn't sure, anymore, which twin was the good one and which was the bad one.

She wasn't even sure which twin was which, when she saw them both at the top of the stairs—until she heard Bonnie speak.

"I'm going to refuse the money," Bonnie said.

"You can't," Blythe said. "I have spent the past three hours hanging streamers and baking cupcakes, which we had to decorate by candlelight after the power went out—"

"And how much did Mommy and Daddy pay you for that?"

"More than I make at the bookstore, that's for sure." Blythe's makeup was heavier than Bonnie's. Her chin was firmer. So was her gaze. "The entire family is going to be at the party. You are not going to screw this up."

"I'm not screwing anything up," Bonnie said. "I'm becoming an adult. You're just getting older."

Bonnie went inside. Blythe was about to follow, but Larkin called "Blythe!" and she stopped.

"Do I know you?" Blythe asked.

"No," Larkin said. "Your sister hired me to figure out who was responsible for murdering her, and I'm pretty sure I just did."

"I'm sorry," Blythe said, "did you just say *murder*?"

"Yes," Larkin said. "Do you want to know who I think it was?"

"No," Blythe said. They could hear Bonnie, through the door, making some kind of announcement about technical difficulties.

"Do you want to get the money?" Larkin asked, switching from detective to director. "For your birthday? Because I can help you do that." She remembered what Anni, the full-time freelance writer, had written during their last business planning session. "I'm Larkin Day. I solve everything."

"Am I being pranked?" Blythe asked. "Is this for a podcast? I knew she'd end up doing that podcast with someone else."

There was something, in Blythe's voice, that suggested the podcast idea had been hers; that she was hurt by the idea of Bonnie being content with somebody beside her—and Larkin suddenly understood that she had misunderstood what Blythe really wanted. Bonnie, through the door, had also shifted tactics, switching from talking to counting. Larkin could hear the guided fitness class springing into action, feet and hands bouncing against the sprung floor.

"It's not a podcast," Larkin said, "it's for real." She thought of what she could say to get Blythe to pay attention—but then Blythe's attention shifted towards the one man everyone in Pratincola recognized. "Is that Dr. Jackson?" Blythe asked, pointing over Larkin's shoulder.

"Yep," Ed said, walking between Larkin and Blythe and pushing open the classroom door. "I take Bonnie's class three times a week. Would you two ladies like to join me?"

Larkin trusted Ed—and followed.

Blythe, surprisingly, did the same.

"Hi!" Bonnie called out, as the three latecomers entered the room. "Six, seven, eight, bend and stretch, hands flat on the floor, and now we lower into plank." She looked up as she lowered. "We don't have music today, but I'm leading the class anyway! No excuses, team! Now hover as I count to twenty!"

Elliott and Anni were planked at the back of the room; Larkin hovered next to Anni and heard the story. When Bonnie realized she was locked out of her dashboard, she decided to run the class without the headset. "She also decided to livestream it," Anni said, her breath slightly ragged, "and she tagged the company that runs the classes, so they'd have proof that she didn't miss a session."

"Sounds like she isn't missing a beat," Ed said. "Pun intended."

"Nineteen, twenty!" Bonnie jumped up from her plank and ran to check her phone. "Check it out! We've got over five thousand followers watching us! That just means we need to work five thousand times harder! Are you ready?"

Larkin was, once again, *not ready*. She was wearing jeans, for starters. Also boots, with no socks. But she lowered herself into the first of the 96 lunges, adjusting her back foot as she dropped to give her still-wet boot a better grip against the floor.

"Two, three, four, *up*, two, three, four, *two*, two, three, four, hi Blythe!" Larkin raised her back leg to get a better look, grabbing onto Ed's shoulder as she slipped and swiveled. Bonnie's twin had taken a spot at the front of the room, and Bonnie—still counting—lunged towards her and gave her a livestream-sized hug.

"This is my twin sister Blythe," she said. "It's our birthday! We used to do this vlog together, when we were really young—can you say what you used to say, Blythe?"

Blythe turned her face towards Bonnie's phone. "Be sure to like and subscribe!"

Bonnie turned back to the class—but Blythe kept talking. "My twin sister thinks she's too old for birthday presents. How many of you think she's wrong? Thumbs up for birthday presents, everybody!"

"*Nineteen*, two three four, *twenty*, two three four—"

"The livestream's, like, *exploding* with thumbs," Blythe

called out, smiling in the exact same way Bonnie had smiled when Larkin first met her. "I think they like me."

"Let's stay focused, three four—"

"Do you want more Bonnie stories?" Blythe asked the phone. "Because I've got 'em. How many of you have been following Bonnie since she first started teaching? Did you know she only expects five percent of you to change your lives and get fit? The rest of you are just watching from home and, like, eating chips. Thumbs up if you're eating chips right now!"

"I like chips!" Bonnie said. "There's room for every kind of food in a healthy diet." She turned back to the class. "Who's ready for high knees?"

"Thumbs up if you're high right now!" Blythe said to the phone. "Thumbs up if you've got your pants unbuttoned! Thumbs up if you've got one hand inside your pants!"

"Thumbs up if you're getting fit!" Larkin called out, from the back of the classroom. "Like me!" She ran to the front of the room and faced the phone. "I'm not the world's skinniest person. I'm not super athletic. But when I started Bonnie's class, I couldn't do lunges or push-ups or any of those things, and now I can."

Larkin used every acting technique she still remembered to keep her breathing steady. "There are all kinds of people in this class, and all kinds of people watching. That's okay. You can look like me—"

"Or you can look like me," Ed said, coming forward and finishing the sentence.

"Or me!" Beth—the newest student—said, giving Larkin and Ed a big sweaty hug. "I made this class my New Year's Resolution, and I haven't missed a single one."

Larkin looked for Anni—this would be the time for her to join in, after all—but Anni and Elliott had disappeared.

"And neither have I," Bonnie said, taking control and smiling at Larkin. "So let's all do high knees together. Does everybody have a buddy?"

Ed looked at Larkin, who nodded him towards Beth. That left one person without a partner.

"Blythe," Larkin asked, "be my buddy?"

Larkin didn't give Blythe the chance to respond. Instead, she stood in front of her and began running in place. "You were the one who deactivated Bonnie's accounts," Larkin said, keeping her voice low and pulling her right and left knees as high as they could go. "But it wasn't your idea."

Talking during high knees was extremely difficult.

"You wouldn't have done it if he hadn't paid you."

It was also extremely difficult to run in place while wearing wet boots. With no socks.

"You can still undo it." Larkin's knees weren't as high as they had been—and her wrist had started bleeding again. "The two of you can be *Blithe and Bonnie* again, if you want, or Bonnie can run the accounts by herself. You just—"

"What," Blythe said, her eyes as flat as her vowels. "Give up the $5 grand?"

"You could still get the money, maybe. If that's what really matters. You could also be good with Bonnie again. You could do that podcast with her. You could do something just for you. You can go after anything you want, Blythe." Larkin was careful not to say that Blythe could get anything she wanted. Neither life nor theater worked that way. "You just have to have a difficult conversation with your sister," Larkin said, her voice hitching as she shifted feet. "And then you have to have a difficult conversation with your dad."

Her left foot came down; her right knee came up.

Larkin watched as a giant drop of blood fell from her right wrist and soaked its way into her jeans, and then her right foot came down again.

And so did the rest of her.

And this time it really, really hurt.

CHAPTER 24

"When they said the fitness class was *sliding scale*," Ed teased, "they didn't mean *slip and slide*."

Larkin and Ed were in the Emergency Room. They had been in the Emergency Room for about an hour, during which time they had learned that Larkin's situation was not critical—"we'll do an X-ray to confirm the ankle isn't broken," the intake nurse had said—and got critical information about what had happened after Blythe took over the livestream.

First, Elliott had killed the Wi-Fi to the entire building.

"I could see disaster coming," he told them, "and I didn't want Bonnie to have a disaster on her record." Elliott and Anni had sat with Ed and Larkin, in the ER waiting room, until both Ed and Larkin told them to go home. "So I figured the best way to stop the livestream was to take down the internet."

This meant that the official recorded component of Bonnie's class ended after Blythe asked the viewers whether they liked birthday presents. The cut was timed, almost perfectly, to "I think they like me!"

"Nobody would think twice about a livestream that stopped working in the middle of a session," Elliott explained. "Real-time video is notoriously unreliable."

"Especially during National Weather Service warning-level snowstorms," Anni added.

The unofficial recorded component began about a minute later. It had been taken by Beth's son, the recalci-trant preteen who always sat in the corner with his phone. Everyone had forgotten about him—Larkin couldn't remember the last time she'd remembered him being there —but apparently he'd accompanied his mother to every class.

He accompanied his video, as well—with piano, auto-tuning, and commentary. He'd done all of this in less time than it took for Larkin and Ed to get admitted to the ER, and now Larkin's "I'm not the world's skinniest person" was followed with "you can take this class if you're fat" and Ed's "You could look like me!" with "you can take this class if you're jacked." When his mom said "I haven't missed a single one," he sang "you can take this class if you're a single mom, just put your kid in the back"—and by the time Bonnie joined the chorus, he had somehow combined the four voices into a bizarre harmony.

The ten-second video had not yet gone viral, but during the time it took for Larkin to get her X-ray, it had amassed another 10,000 views—including a thumbs-up from the fitness company. "We love Bonnie Cooper," was the official comment, from the official account, "and we love that fitness is for everyone!"

"Well," Larkin said, "I think Bonnie's job is safe."

That was when Nate, the nurse, entered the room.

Larkin had met Nate during her first murder investigation. He was delighted to see her again, even under less-than-optimal circumstances. "We got the results," Nate said. "The ankle isn't broken, just sprained. That means I get to wrap you up and prescribe RICE." He smiled at Larkin. "That's one of the few things a nurse can prescribe!"

"What about painkillers?" Larkin asked. "Can we get a doctor to get us some of those?"

"There is no P in RICE," Nate said, the words falling out of his mouth as if he had said them many times before. "Take the P, pay the PRICE."

"Fine," Larkin said. When she'd first met Nate, she had asked him about opiate abuse in the Midwest—and she knew he had seen many situations in which pain medication created more problems than it solved. "I can have an aspirin, right?"

"If you want," Nate said. "But when I finish wrapping this ankle, you may not need one."

That was when he noticed Larkin's wrist. "Are you bleeding? Is that on your intake form?" He examined Larkin's wrist and immediately applied a stinging, sterilizing wipe. "That cut has got to be an inch long, and the edges are all jagged."

"I fell on a decorative rock border," Larkin said. "In the snow." She was pretty sure that was what had happened. A lot had happened since she woke up that morning, and it was only—she checked the clock on the wall—6:45.

"Yeah, a rock could have done that," Nate said. "Which means you get to stick around here until I can stitch you up."

Nate left, presumably to do whatever medical bureaucratic procedures were required before he could come back and apply dissolving thread to Larkin's wrist—and Larkin suddenly remembered the other problem she was supposed to have solved that evening.

"Ed," she said, "do you have your phone with you?"

Of course he did.

"Can you see what Ghoti's been up to?"

"I really shouldn't be checking my students' social media feeds," Ed said—but he did, and he handed the phone to Larkin so she could see what Ghoti had done.

A hashtag:

#OhDeanMyDean.

A series of signs:

Dean Day helped me apply for my first internship.

Dean Day does everything she can to improve Howell's campus.

Dean Day's office has the best coffee.

There was a reply to that one—a copycat sign, a snarkier student, *Dean Day brings her coffee from home because campus coffee is so bad*—but overall the campaign was positive. Ghoti had successfully recruited several Howell students to post nice things about Dean Day, and had even more successfully copied, pasted, and remixed their posts to turn the last-minute hashtag into an hour-long movement.

There weren't a lot of posts, but there were enough to counterbalance the single photo Janessa had taken of the six signs. Janessa had recruited five other students to post one negative sentence; Ghoti had gotten at least twenty-five other students to create a wave of positive sentiment.

It had worked.

Larkin Day had, in fact, solved everything—with Ghoti's help, and Anni's, and Elliott's, and Ed's, and now Nate's, who had returned to stitch her wrist together.

"Did I see Anni with a gentleman friend?" Nate asked. He had once had a crush on Anni. He probably still did.

"Yes," Ed said. "His name's Elliott Fox." This seemed like the kind of conversation that was best handled man-to-man, so Larkin stayed out of it. "He's going to be sticking around Pratincola for a while, I think."

"That's what I thought," Nate said. He smiled again, trying to hide his disappointment. "Well, at least I'll get to help you and Anni write your musical."

"Right," Larkin said. During her first murder investigation, she had told Nate that she and Anni were writing a musical together. It hadn't been true—she had just done it as an excuse to ask Nate about how certain types of drugs worked—and Anni had warned her that Nate would ask about that musical every time he saw them. Anni had, once again, been right.

"We're still thinking about it," Larkin said. "I was thinking maybe we could do one of those things where you turn a classic movie into a musical."

"That's a great idea," Nate said. "Those always make so much money."

"But it's going to take forever to get the rights," Larkin said. "So we probably won't get started right away. Plus, you have to make sure nobody else is already doing the movie you want. What if you do an entire first draft and then find out that Lin-Manuel Miranda is already working on *Dead Poets Society*?"

"I thought Lin-Manuel Miranda was doing Disney stuff," Nate said. "And if you're going to do *DPS*, you have to change the ending." He gave Larkin's wrist a final examination and stood up. "It would be a big number, right? All of those students standing on their desks?"

"Probably," Larkin said. She swore—*shiitake mushrooms*—that she would never lie to anybody about writing a musical ever again.

"And then, what?" Nate asked. "Mr. Keating resigns anyway?"

Larkin looked quickly at Ed. He looked quickly at Nate. "We have to go," Ed said. "Tell us what we need to do so that we can take Larkin home."

CHAPTER 25

E d helped Larkin up the unshoveled sidewalk. He kissed her—first on her left cheek, and then, tentatively, the left corner of her mouth—and said "I know we were going to hang out at my place and talk about stuff, but it's been a long day. How about we postpone our conversation until after we both get some rest?"

"Only if I also get ice, compression, and elevation," Larkin said. "And a cup of coffee."

They kissed again, their lips uncertain, hesitant to answer a question that had not yet been asked. It was not their best kiss. It was, perhaps, their most honest one.

"Go inside," Ed said. "Tell your mother she contains multitudes."

Larkin watched Ed walk back to his car. Then she opened her mother's front door.

Josephine Day was in the kitchen, at her usual seat. Her coffee cup was to her right. Her tablet was to her left. The sound was on, and Larkin—as she hobbled carefully through the living room—recognized both the voice and the video.

It was the footage of Elliott's disaster, back when he was Scarbo. The flames, the blackout, the fall; everything they had watched together, before. Larkin's mother was watching the part that came afterwards—the part that had actually ended Elliott's network television career.

The part where Scarbo apologized.

"It would be foolish of me to say it were anyone else's fault," Elliott said, through her mother's tablet. "It would also be easy. Blame my manager for insisting I expand my repertoire. Blame the theater for not giving us adequate rehearsal time. Blame the network and its continuous demands for growth."

This was, of course, unscripted. That was not why it was unforgivable.

"I am no fool," Elliott said. "I am a magician. I am also an adult who, for the past year, has behaved like a child. Saying yes when I should have said no, to please the people who handed out paychecks and presents. Taking what I had not earned, so that someone else could take more. Avoiding all kinds of work, especially the kind of work that would make it less likely for people to *like me*."

He must have understood that his audience wouldn't understand any of this—or like it. They laughed, instead; Larkin's mother's tablet had already queued up three late-night parodies of Elliott's disastrous speech.

"You might say I let myself be manipulated. I will simply respond that a true magician is fully responsible for *every single manipulation*. Including the one you just saw."

He snapped his fingers.

"*Et soudain il s'éteignait.*"

Then he walked off the stage.

"And he was extinguished," Josephine said, looking up and seeing Larkin. "But he seems to be doing fine now."

"Yeah," Larkin said. "I mean, I'd have to ask Anni about it, but programmers tend to land on their feet." She gestured towards her wrapped ankle. "I, on the other hand, landed on my butt." Then she showed her mother her other hand, with its stitched-up wrist. "Twice."

"My poor baby," Josephine said, getting up to inspect Larkin's bandages. "You're all right, though? Nothing broken?"

"All I need is RICE," Larkin said. "And coffee." She sat down, taking off her boots. "And a fresh pair of socks, because my old pair ended up in Ed's car, so did your gloves, I'm sorry—"

"That's the least of my concerns, right now—"

"But I'll get the gloves back, and if you could please cut me one of those brownies to go with the coffee, you would be the best mother ever." Larkin twitched her nose at her mother.

Josephine twitched her nose back. "Let me see what I can do."

As her mother provided socks, a pillow for Larkin's foot, another pillow for Larkin's wrist, and a brownie that was nearly as large as Larkin's uninjured hand, Larkin caught her mother up on the events of the day.

"I saw that fitness video, the one the kid made," Josephine said, handing Larkin her coffee and sitting down. "I don't even know why I saw it. It just showed up in my social media feed when I was looking at my hashtag."

"Wow," Larkin said. "I guess it's trending."

"My daughter is trending!" Larkin's mother said. "I'm so proud."

"What did you think of the hashtag, though?" Larkin asked. "Oh dean, my dean?"

Josephine tapped at her tablet, turning it off. "Your

friend Elliott makes a very good apology," she said. "He knows what to say, how to say it, and when to walk away."

Larkin hoped her mother was making a *non sequitur*, not changing the subject. "Didn't you like that all of those Howell students said such nice things about you?"

"Yes," Josephine said. It sounded a little noncommittal.

"And the posts totally bumped out all of the ones Janessa made," Larkin said.

"I don't know what that means," Josephine said, "but yes."

"It means you can still be Dean," Larkin said. "For as long as you want."

"Larkin." Her mother stood up again. She walked towards the living room and looked out the window at where the signs had been. "I told Arnold that I was going to resign at the end of the academic year."

Larkin almost stood up—but it hurt too much. The whole thing. "You're resigning?"

"I have to," Josephine said.

"But they're not going to let Janessa—"

"Of course not," Josephine said, turning around and walking back into the kitchen. "Although Arnold had to call the Board first, so they could be the ones who officially rejected Janessa's plan. That man has got no spine, and that young woman has got some nerve—and it'll do her good one of these days, but today is not that day." She picked up the coffeepot, thought better of it, and poured herself a glass of water. "They're going to do a search for a dean with the appropriate credentials."

"Why not you?"

"Because I'm no longer sure I have the appropriate credentials." Larkin's mother sat down. She looked at Larkin—and for the first time in Larkin's life, she felt like her mother was seeing her as an adult. Even though Larkin was eating a brownie and sitting with a stitched-up wrist and a wrapped-up ankle. Even though she had lost her phone—and her mother didn't even know about *that,* yet—and left her mother's gloves in Ed's car, and left her own car parked outside of the Howell bookstore.

Even though she had failed to solve her mother's problem.

But her mother appeared to have solved the problem on her own.

"Janessa was right about a few things," Josephine said. "Maybe more than a few things. I don't know what today's students want, that's for sure." She took a sip of her water. "I looked up that poem she mentioned. The one about the tiger, that the six-year-old wrote. It's really good!"

"All right," Larkin said, in one final attempt to solve everything, "so I'll show you all the best memes and then you can still be Dean."

"No," Josephine said. "The other reason I can't be Dean is because I let too many things happen on my watch. I got so distracted by departmental politics—whether or not to hold Pancake Breakfast, for example—that I missed a literal coup!"

"You can't let Janessa—"

"I could have prevented that," Josephine said, "if I had been at all sensitive to what the student body was thinking." She stood up again. "And, all right, *feeling*." She was circling the table, squeezing herself against the counter so as not to bump either of Larkin's chairs. "I *am* out of touch, and it would probably be better to hire someone who was younger and had a shared *lived experience*—those are the words, right?—with an underserved segment of our student body. Not that you want to pick somebody simply because of their background, you need to look at the entire value-add, but—well, look at me! I'm talking about Howell in terms like *value-add*. The students are talking about Howell in terms of *impact* and *equity* and *a more progressive future*."

Josephine paused, and looked towards the front window again. "I just don't see that future being led by someone like me." She turned back towards her daughter. "And neither do they."

"What are you going to do?" Larkin asked.

"I'm probably going to teach," her mother said. "There's plenty of room for people like me in the private tutoring market." She twitched her nose at Larkin. "But we don't have to think about that until this summer. Maybe longer. Howell owes me a sabbatical, so I negotiated it into a semester's worth of severance."

Larkin twitched her nose back. "Yay?"

Josephine smiled. "We'll say *yay*."

They sat, two adults, side by side.

"Hey," Larkin said, when she remembered. "If you're no longer going to be Ed's boss, can I tell you what he said about you?"

"You could have told me anyway," Josephine said. "I recused myself from his tenure committee in November."

"He said you contain multitudes."

"Another Whitman," Larkin's mother said.

"Is that the one where you celebrate yourself and sing yourself?"

"Yes," Josephine said. "But the part Ed is quoting comes from the section in which you contradict yourself. One must be either incomplete or inconsistent, as the mathematicians say." She picked up Larkin's empty coffee mug. "I think the poets say it better." She picked up Larkin's empty plate. "You do know that *O Captain! My*

Captain! is a eulogy, right? For Abraham Lincoln? Most people just know the first line. Even those Howell students, making those posts online—I can't imagine any of them understanding that they were invoking a funeral."

"No," Larkin said. "I'm pretty sure at least one of them knew exactly what they were doing." She let her mother help her up and walk her towards the guest bedroom. "You really should get to know Ghoti, while you still have the chance. I think they're the kind of student you've always wanted to help."

"I already have," Josephine said. "Ghoti is going to be my new assistant, now that my previous student-leader has proven herself unsuitable for the job. It'll only be for a few months, but if they do well, maybe the next dean will want to keep them on."

Larkin let her mother hunt around the piles of washed and unwashed clothes for a fresh set of pajamas. She let her mother fold the pajamas neatly and place them on the corner of Larkin's unmade bed. That single gesture, from mother to daughter, turned the room from *the guest bedroom* to *Larkin's room*—which meant that Larkin should probably take better care of it, in the future.

Adults were responsible, after all.

So was her mother.

"The past and present wilt," Josephine said, standing in the doorway and reciting poetry just like she had when Larkin was a child. "I have fill'd them, emptied them, and proceed to fill my next fold of the future."

CHAPTER 26

"Tell them how you did it, Blythe."

"I will—but first we need to share a special message from one of our sponsors."

Larkin was walking the track on the second floor of the Pratincola Fitness Complex. Nate had given her permission to resume light exercise. He also told her that *Dead Poets Society* had already been turned into a play, and suggested that she and Anni start working on something new.

Blythe and Bonnie were also working on something new—and Larkin let the podcast episode continue without tapping the button that would skip the commercial. Her phone still worked, despite its exposure to a National Weather Service warning-level snowstorm. Larkin had found it, safe and sound, in a Howell lost-and-found box —and vowed never to let it slip from her fingers again.

"Are you an influencer?" Blythe asked.

"Yes!" Bonnie said. "You can follow me at *Blithe and Bonnie* on social."

"Hey," Blythe said, "that's my name! Does that make me an influencer too?"

"Yes, it does," Bonnie said, "and influencers work better when they work together."

This was the opening of a two-minute ad for Sharefluence, a new app developed by a Cedar Rapids-based startup. "It's like a dating app," Bonnie said, "except it connects influencers."

"So they can promote each other's work!" Blythe finished.

Larkin remembered Bonnie referencing this app. It had been at the beginning of class—and if Larkin remembered correctly, it had happened while Blythe was in the classroom, ending Bonnie's online life. It was interesting to think about everything she'd missed. It was also interesting to think about the ways in which everything circled back, the way she was circling the track, the way Blythe and Bonnie were making content again. The way her mother was teaching again—or would be, once the transition was complete.

But Larkin was still in transition, every step a little more painful than she was expecting—and so she would distract herself, as people did, with podcasts.

"After Christmas," Blythe said, "Dad offered me two grand to take you down."

"Two Gs?" Bonnie sounded a little surprised—and a little envious. "Gee, Blythe, he must have really wanted to keep me from using my phone at family gatherings."

"It wasn't just that," Blythe said. "You had become this person we didn't recognize. You were changing your life, and making all of these decisions, and getting involved in all kinds of new things, and you weren't bringing any of us along."

"I know," Bonnie said. "I thought I was growing up, but I was actually growing apart."

"From me."

"From you."

Larkin wondered how much of this was scripted. She wondered if they'd hired someone else to write the script.

"And that's why I took the money," Blythe said. "I mean, I also *really, really needed the money*. But I could have found another way to earn it. Instead, I took what you had created."

"But it was yours, too!" Bonnie said. "We made the first *Blithe and Bonnie* accounts together."

"I know!" Blythe said. "Which was why it was so easy for me to take them down."

The technical explanation followed. Blythe had used her face—a twin's face—to unlock Bonnie's phone. From there, she deleted Bonnie's content and deactivated Bonnie's accounts. Then she used Bonnie's password manager to change all of Bonnie's existing passwords, signed herself out of Bonnie's email and cloud storage accounts, and reset Bonnie's phone to its factory settings. She'd already reset Bonnie's laptop, at their apartment—after using Bonnie's email to send a takedown request to the Wayback Machine.

"There are only, like, three ways you can wipe the Wayback Machine," Blythe explained, "and one of them is by proving that you own the content and no longer want it archived."

"Well, you kind of owned the content," Bonnie said. "Some of it, anyway. The stuff we made when we were children."

"Yeah," Blythe said. "We were able to get your followers back when we reactivated your accounts, and you were able to get your email and cloud stuff back by calling customer service and reciting some old passwords that I had no idea you still had memorized—"

"I'm good at memorizing," Bonnie said. "It's kind of essential, for my job—"

"But I kind of wish I hadn't deleted all of those posts and videos."

"Well," Bonnie said, "have I got a surprise for you—and for our listeners!"

Larkin already knew what the surprise was. She had helped connect Blythe and Bonnie to another person of influence, and she hadn't needed a dating-style app to do it.

"As soon as we get back from our break," Bonnie continued, "we're going to introduce you to Ghoti—that's G-H-O-T-I, in case you're curious—and talk about how they were able to get all of our old videos back online."

"But first!" Blythe said again. "A word from one of our sponsors."

"Blythe!" Bonnie laughed—and Larkin pulled out her phone and rewound ten seconds, because it sounded like Bonnie's real laugh. "You mean *a word from us*, about one of our sponsors."

"And it's the same sponsor you heard from, I mean *heard from us from*, before," Blythe said, laughing in the exact same way, "because until this podcast gets a few more followers, we only have the one!"

"So be sure to like—"

"And subscribe."

———

"Would you like a cup of coffee," Anni asked, when the two of them met up for their weekly business planning session, "or would you like an Energy Drink?"

She held out the bottle to Larkin.

"Drink's life-changing nutritional solution," Larkin read aloud, "now with caffeine!"

"Bonnie was giving these out to everyone after class," Anni explained. "The room was packed, by the way. I think they're going to start offering more sessions."

It had only been a week since Bonnie's class had gone viral—but after Beth's son's video made it first to the social media feeds and then to the morning news shows, attendance had gone way up. So had Bonnie's sponsorship opportunities. In addition to Drink, she was now making content for a shoe company and a meditation app. Plus, she'd landed Sharefluence, which had agreed to sponsor Blythe and Bonnie's podcast in exchange for access to Bonnie's much larger fitness audience. Only 5% of Bonnie's followers wanted to get fit, the Sharefluence CEOs explained, but at least 50% dreamed of becoming influencers.

Bonnie had shared all of this with Larkin over email, now that she'd gotten her email back. She'd also asked Larkin to send an invoice for her services.

"Which I don't think I can do, right?" Larkin asked Anni, coffee in one hand and Energy Drink in the other. "I mean, I have to become a business before I can send an invoice."

The Energy Drink tasted like a liquid gummy vitamin that had picked up a bunch of metal filings somewhere. Larkin put it down and continued to sip her coffee. "And I didn't really solve her murder. Elliott and Ghoti were the ones who helped Bonnie get back online."

"But you solved the problem," Anni said. "You got Blythe and Bonnie back together, and you got the two of them to talk to their parents, and that is all that matters."

She looked at the notebook that she always carried with her. "Did they get the birthday money?"

"I don't know," Larkin said. "I didn't ask."

Anni raised an eyebrow.

"I thought it would be rude!" Larkin had been thinking, since Anni's letter, about how to ask better questions. It would make her a better friend. It would also make her a better detective. It might even make her a better girlfriend.

Larkin had already told Anni about her conversation with Ed. "I found out about the whole Thanksgiving thing," she'd said, two days ago, the two of them sitting on Larkin's freshly made bed. Larkin had invited Anni to her home, first because it felt unfair to make Anni do all the hosting and second because she had started thinking of it as *home*. "Did you know Ed has a brother?"

"Yes." It always surprised Larkin, how much Anni knew.

"Well, apparently Ed's brother is really, really successful, owns his own construction company, beautiful wife, beautiful kids, the whole bit." Larkin had met them all at Ed's family's Thanksgiving dinner, and they were exactly as described. "And here's Ed, the kid brother, who doesn't have a real job yet—"

"He's an assistant professor!"

"Sure," Larkin said, "but until you get tenure, you're still auditioning."

"Nobody can look at Ed and think he isn't successful," Anni said.

"But he doesn't have a house," Larkin said, "and he isn't married, and he hasn't produced any grandkids." She took a drink of coffee at that point—if she remembered correctly—and continued. "So he produced *me*."

"Ah," Anni said, understanding. "You weren't there

because Ed wanted you to be there. You were there so Ed could show his family that he was leveling up."

"And he felt awful about it," Larkin said, "so he just, like, clammed up afterwards."

"Some men do that," Anni said. "Probably people do it regardless of gender, but it's a behavior that's often associated with cisgender men."

"Well," Larkin said, "I didn't know what was going on." She was quite sure she took another sip of coffee. It would have been the right time to do it. "And Ed didn't know how to solve his problem, which he described as *the problem of not knowing how to be Ed*, until he and I started talking about it."

"I'd ask you if you helped him figure it out," Anni said, "except I already know that's not the kind of problem you can solve in a single conversation."

"Not even with Larkin Day on your team," Larkin said.

"So you are a team?" Anni asked. "You and Ed?"

"Not in the way that you and Elliott are a team," Larkin said. "And not in the way that Mom and Claire are a team. But we're going to keep making things together, and we're going to see what happens."

"Good," Anni had said, because it was.

"How are you and Elliott doing?" Larkin continued— both *then*, when she and Anni had sat together in her bedroom, and *now*, when she and Anni were sitting together in Anni's apartment.

Anni smiled. Then she blushed. Then she got up and began misting her plants. "He's driving back from Champaign-Urbana tonight, because we're going to Ben and Mitchell's Valentine's Day party tomorrow. Then he's going to stay in Pratincola for a week or two while we start hunting for a place that's large enough for both of us."

"That fast?"

"Neither of us are procrastinators," Anni said. "Unlike a certain unlicensed private detective who has yet to finish her business plan."

Larkin watched as Anni adjusted one of the trailing vines on what might have been a philodendron. Or a pothos plant. Anni had both, and they were hard to tell apart. "I could blame it on my ankle," she said, "but the truth is that I'm not sure I really want to become a licensed private detective."

Anni put her plant mister back where it belonged. "I know," she said.

"I still kinda want to do theater."

"I know," Anni said again. "You know you can do both, right?"

"Yeah," Larkin said. "Which is what I should be doing, but there's no way I can do theater rehearsals until 11 in the evening and then get up for a 6 a.m. shift at The Coffee Shop, and there's no way I can stop being a barista until I get my private detective business set up, and I don't want to get my private detective business set up until I figure out how to balance it with the theater thing."

That was a lie.

"I mean, I don't want to get my private detective business set up until I figure out whether there's any possibility of still doing theater professionally."

That was the truth. It was also *what Larkin wanted*, which meant she could start working towards it.

"Well," Anni said, "now that you've finally said it—and I have been waiting for you to say this for *nearly two months*, by the way—we can close out our weekly business planning sessions and transition them into weekly friendship sessions." She sat down next to Larkin and tucked her feet under her knees. "Can you help me find something to wear to Ben and Mitchell's party?"

———

The four of them—Ed, Larkin, Elliott, and Anni—sat comfortably together in Ben and Mitchell's living room. Ben was pouring the wine; Elliott and Mitchell were having an impossible-to-follow conversation about programming languages.

"You didn't tell me he was an engineer," Ben said, picking up his glass and positioning himself on the ottoman in front of Anni. "That's even better than being, you know, whoever it was he used to be."

"Whomever," Anni said. Then she corrected herself. "Sorry. I'm trying to get better at talking to people, and that was not very good." She sipped her wine. "I should have said *we're all constantly becoming better than the people we used to be.*"

"Some of us, anyway," Ed said.

"And some of us are still trying to figure out who to become," Larkin said.

"I'd drink to that," Ben said, "but I think I just heard the doorbell."

Anni, who was wearing a pink dress with tiny red hearts on it—Larkin had tried to talk her into buying something a little more grown-up, but Anni had argued that adults could buy whatever party dresses they wanted —had never been in Ben and Mitchell's mansion before. "I still can't believe he gets his own doorbell," she whispered. "And pours his own wine."

"Why?" Ed whispered back. "Were you expecting a butler?"

Ed was wearing the cashmere sweater Larkin had gotten him for Christmas. The scarf Larkin had given him as a Valentine's Day present was tucked into the left sleeve of his coat. Larkin was wearing heels, fishnet stockings, three different support garments, a blue-and-silver dress that glittered under Ben and Mitchell's chandelier, and the four-pendant necklace Ed had given her for Valentine's Day.

One pendant was shaped like a tiny magnifying glass.

One pendant was shaped like a pair of theater masks.

One pendant was shaped like a cup of coffee.

One pendant was shaped like a question mark.

It was perfect.

The entire evening had been perfect.

And then Ben returned, with two new guests—one of whom Larkin immediately recognized.

"You remember Sahil Malhotra," Ben said, "and his wife, Rupa."

"Of course," Larkin said, standing up, wobbling on her heels and her still-healing ankle. She didn't really remember Rupa, but she had spent the entirety of Ben and Mitchell's New Year's Eve dinner seated next to Sahil. "We spoke about Shakespeare."

"*Romeo and Juliet.*" Sahil smiled at Larkin. He was about Mitchell's age; one of Mitchell's business partners, if Larkin remembered correctly. Rupa was a doctor. They were both impeccably dressed. "I shared your insights at our most recent Summer Shakespeare planning session. They were very well received, as was your resume."

"My resume?" Larkin was confused. "You mean the one on my website?" She had been meaning to update her professional website since October; to remove her theatrical credits and replace them with information on how to hire her as a private investigator. Of course, she would have had to become a private investigator first, business license and all—and for once, she was glad she had procrastinated.

"Don't act like you're surprised," Ben said. "I told you Sahil was looking to meet young, interesting directors."

Ben had, in fact, said something very like that on New Year's Eve, before he led Larkin to her place setting. He had also said that he would make sure she and Ed got their kiss at midnight, and she had forgotten about everything else that came before.

"We'd like you to meet the team next week," Sahil said, "to see if you'd be a good fit to direct *Romeo and Juliet* this summer. You'd need to start right away, of course—we've got an office in Cedar Rapids that you can use, and we'll be holding auditions the first week of April."

"I'm sorry," Larkin said, "I wasn't expecting any of this."

"To be fair," Mitchell said, standing up and joining Larkin and Sahil, "it was a little last-minute."

"The previous director got caught touching someone's diaphragm," Ed explained.

"Not a student's, right?"

"No, thank goodness," Ed said. "But not his wife's."

"So you'll be taking over an eight-month contract," Sahil continued, "a month-and-a-half in. But you should be very happy with the compensation. The Summer Shakespeare project is funded by some very generous sponsors, one of whom is standing right next to you."

"You're welcome," Mitchell said.

"I didn't even interview," Larkin said.

"You didn't need to," Mitchell said. "I've been watching you work with Ben on his opera for months."

"And here I was," Ben teased, "thinking you were watching *me*."

"Don't you need to have a national search?" Larkin asked. "Aren't there rules about this?"

"There are," Mitchell said, "but the Board reserves the

right to recommend a director of their choosing if there is no time to conduct a national search. That said, we will need to conduct one next year—which means that you'll have to re-interview, formally, in the fall."

"And then if we hire you, formally," Sahil continued, "it will be January through August, renewable every year as long as we still agree we're a good fit."

"Most of the directors use the semester break to teach," Ed explained.

"But you can use it to solve murders!" Anni said, toasting Larkin with her empty glass of wine.

"You solve murders?" This was from Rupa, who stepped between her husband and Mitchell to take her place in what was now the most interesting part of the conversation. "Actual murders?"

"Well, my most recent case wasn't exactly a *murder-murder*," Larkin said. "I mean, there wasn't a dead body."

"But there were a lot of dead social media accounts," Elliott said. His tie was pink, purchased to match Anni's dress. "And Larkin solved the whole thing—in just a week!"

"Because Larkin Day solves everything," Anni said.

"And now you get to solve the case of *how to direct Summer Shakespeare*," Ed said, "with me as your musical director." He turned to Larkin and took her hand. "Are you ready?"

"Yes," Larkin said, squeezing Ed's hand. "I'm ready."

Larkin may think she's switched from detecting to directing, but there are surprises in store as she and Ed spend their summer dealing with doublets, couplets, Capulets, and corpses. SHAKE-SPEARE IN THE PARK WITH MURDER releases Summer 2023!

AUTHOR'S NOTE

It is the penultimate day of November. The last warm day we may have, for the remainder of the year. I am writing this outside, in what remains of the garden Larry and I planted this summer; the rest of the garden has been transplanted indoors, to accompany our daily piano practice and our nightly conversations.

I forget whether it was Larry or I who first opened the conversation of *how to write the Larkin books as if they were art*. I remember that we both agreed that *what made a book art* was difficult to define. I mentioned Manjula Martin's interview with Jonathan Franzen, which you can read in Martin's anthology *Scratch: Writers, Money, and the Art of Making a Living*, because Franzen told Martin that the best way to determine whether you were about to read a "serious novel" (his words) was to look at the first five pages and count the clichés.

I don't believe there are any clichés in the first five pages of *Like, Subscribe, and Murder*—and if there are, you can email me.

But I also don't believe that eliminating phrases like

"quiet as a mouse" (Franzen's words, again) necessarily makes writing serious, or artistic, or any of the things Larry and I knew we both meant when we agreed that I should continue working to bring each successive *Larkin Day Mystery* as close to this undefinable standard as possible.

Larry would argue that the standard is definable; we just haven't figured out how to define it yet. There's a reason why Beethoven's Ninth Symphony is a more cohesive work than his Fifth and why Shakespeare's *Romeo and Juliet* holds together better than *A Midsummer Night's Dream*. It's the combination of *what is known* and *what is new*, perhaps—without any extraneous material that does not directly affect that specific connection.

But I won't use this space to elaborate on the parts of *A Midsummer Night's Dream* that directors always cut, or the parts of Beethoven's Fifth that conductors always rush through.

Instead, I'll give you one small example of how I made *Like, Subscribe, and Murder* a better book than *Ode to Murder*.

There are many reasons why *LSM* is a stronger novel than *OTM*. The first *Larkin Day Mystery* was a pilot episode, if you'll forgive the comparison. The second mystery both complicates the characters and raises the stakes. It introduces an additional level of complexity, allowing readers who have already finished the first book to experience the cognitive thrill of integrating *what they knew* (about Larkin, Anni, Ed, and Josephine) with *something new*. The third book gets even more complicated—and, just in case you were curious, will have at least *two dead bodies*.

But back to my example. One of the reasons why *LSM* is closer to the not-yet-definable ideal comes at the end of the chapter where Anni and Larkin discuss relationships. The penultimate draft of the chapter—the one that made it as far as the proofreader, before I figured out how to fix it —ended on an entirely different metaphor.

Here is what Anni originally said:

> "You're missing the point. We could have, and we didn't, because we didn't understand that relationships were something you *made*. We thought relationships were these things you put on, like a jacket, and if the jacket doesn't fit you either feel uncomfortable or get rid of it, and at least we were both smart enough to choose *not uncomfortable*."

That section of the book kept bothering me, because the idea I gave to Anni wasn't my idea. I got it from a Captain Awkward column titled "How is this relationship like ill-fitting pants?" and although it wasn't so close as to be plagiarism it felt like the wrong choice. It was someone else's simile, a shortcut shoved into Anni's mouth, when I could have given Anni a metaphor that *only she could have come up with*.

And, finally, I did. In the final draft, Anni Morgan, the full-time finance writer who dropped the *e* from her name to improve her presence in search results, says this:

> "You're missing the point. We could have, and we didn't, because we didn't understand that relationships were something you *made*. We thought relationships were these things you bought into, like an index fund, and if the relationship doesn't follow the growth curve you were hoping for, you transfer your assets to someone else."

Books are something you make, too. They aren't these things you put together out of other people's ideas; if they follow a structure that has already been proved to work, like star-crossed lovers or the murder mystery plot, they have to combine *origin* and *original* in a way that invites readers to take a new journey along an old path.

The best books—the ones that qualify as *art*, perhaps— take this invitation even further, turning the old structure into a new standard.

I'll tell that to Larry, tonight—but I told it to you first, on the second-to-last day of the second-to-last month of 2022.

Nicole

ACKNOWLEDGMENTS

Thanks to Alan, Erin, my parents, and Larry, all of whom read various versions of the book and offered extremely helpful guidance.

Thanks to you for reading this version.

Now go read everything else Shortwave Publishing has published.

ABOUT THE AUTHOR

Nicole Dieker is a writer, teacher, and musician. She began her writing career as a full-time freelancer with a focus on personal finance and habit formation; she launched her fiction career with *The Biographies of Ordinary People,* a definitely-not-autobiographical novel that follows three sisters from 1989 to 2016.

Currently, Dieker writes the *Larkin Day* mystery series and the perzine *WHAT IT IS and WHAT TO DO NEXT.* She also maintains an active freelance career; her work has appeared in Vox, Morning Brew, Lifehacker, Bankrate, Haven Life, Popular Science, and more. Dieker spent five years as writer and editor for The Billfold, a personal finance blog where people had honest conversations about money.

Praise from Kirkus Reviews: "Dieker excels at depicting how real people think and act."

Dieker lives in Quincy, Illinois with the great love of her life, his piano, and their garden.